LOTIONS, POTIONS, AND SLIME: MUDPIES AND MORE!

by Nancy Blakey

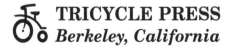

TRICYCLE PRESS
Berkeley, California

If we kept the natural instincts to touch and hum and doodle intact,
we'd all be healthier human beings.

—DONNA PORTER

TRICYCLE PRESS
P.O. Box 7123
Berkeley, California 94707

Illustrations by Melissah Watts

Library of Congress Cataloging-in-Publication Data

Blakey, Nancy.
    Lotions, potions, and slime: mudpies and more! / by Nancy Blakey.
        p. cm
    Summary: A collection of creative activities involving science, art, cooking,
and concocting.
    ISBN 1-883672-21-X
    1. Handicraft—Juvenile literature. 2. Science—Experiments—Juvenile
literature. 3. Cookery—Juvenile literature. [1. Handicraft. 2. Science—
Experiments. 3. Experiments. 4. Cookery.] I. Title.
TT160.B48 1996   95-41082
790.1'922—dc20   CIP
                                                     AC

First Tricycle Press printing, 1996

PRINTED IN CANADA

    2   3   4   5   6   —   01   00   99   98   97   96

For my mudpie makers,
Jenna, Ben, Daniel, and Nicky

Contents

Acknowledgments

A book like this is not possible without the serious play and tomfoolery of many dedicated kids of all ages. A big thank you to: Jenna, Ben, Daniel, and Nicky, Joscelyn, Kevin and Stella, Marti, Jake, Kara, and Greg and Marta—the core engineers who never failed me. And a huge thank you to Barbara Chrisman for her wondrous editing skills.

Making a Mudpie Mess

It was a rainy night. Windy. Cold. Perfect for making a UFO movie, the boys declared. For the class report! they hastily added.

Wait a minute, I said, everyone else is making display boards or giving oral presentations on their research topic.

Too tame, they scoffed. Too boring. And they set to work.

Soon there were stainless-steel bowls, copper wires, batteries, string, and threads of glue everywhere. More boys arrived. More boys to eat supper at the kitchen table and trot their muddy boots in and out of the house between takes. There was noise, disorder, waves of laughter, and flashing green lights. Dogs barked, the phone rang incessantly, the rain fell. Dad came home to bedlam. Why couldn't that kid just do a report on Argentina? he asked.

The road through creativity can be a messy one—full of detours and distractions and slippery possibilities. It is this opportunity for mess that frightens parents away from home art projects. Who has the time to provide art ingredients for their kids, carve out a space to do the project, and clean up afterwards?

You do.

Picture a glorious feast. A good body-and-soul kind of meal. The kind with friends and family, where the fragrant remains are idly picked through and nibbled as you laugh and talk and think about dessert. Take a closer look at this feast. The cook had to peel and dice and roast and bake the way to a heavenly meal. There is an avalanche of pots and pans. There are wet counters, flour-strewn corners, peelings and piles of plates everywhere. But you sat down to a feast. A feast you will remember long after the dishes are done.

Do away with the mess. Get rid of all that work—eat boxed macaroni and cheese. Or peanut butter sandwiches. Better yet—TV dinners! No mess. No fuss.

And no feast either.

Imagination is a feast—scissors and paper and clay and crayons are the tools that take you there. Your child could survive just fine with a few coloring books and school art and an occasional craft class where someone else besides you cleans up afterwards. But the truth is, home is the seedbed of creativity. It is where games are played, birthday cakes are baked, and pumpkins are carved. And maybe the games are played with invented rules, or the cake is purple frosted with great green jelly beans on top. Maybe the pumpkin is carved a month before Halloween and becomes a martian or a tic-tac-toe face. There is great power and imagination in making ideas happen. Chances are, these ideas won't flower and bear fruit in a classroom alone. *Home* is where creative distractions can lead one to the true definition of one's self.

A parent's attitude toward creativity in the home can allow that wild and messy feast of a UFO movie, or narrow the options to only one possibility: a written report on Argentina. Your home should be the place where the mess is seen as only an incidental in the larger arena of imagination. You don't become a Picasso or a Spielberg or an Einstein by worrying about being messy. You arrive there by fooling around with your paints or making your family drop everything to act in a home movie, or by playing with numbers and remembering your dreams. There are no shortcuts.

But lest you think I am an exceptionally tolerant parent, I want to confess that I was short-tempered and cranky the night of the UFO movie. I didn't *want* messes or a houseful of boys or to spend precious time picking sharp pieces of copper from my socks. I yelled CLOSE THE DOOR! a million times. I snorted and sighed and tried to put the crazy idea out of their heads. But I am a pushover for passion. Their passion for making an idea happen completely overcame my nattering. I surrendered.

The movie was wonderful. I was proud of their perseverance and energy. Next? (of course there is a next): An action-packed adventure with criminals and fist fights, and by the way Mom don't you have a recipe in one of your books to make fake windows out of melted sugar so they break and look real?

Lotions, Potions, and Slime is a set of creative opportunities. As you browse, remember how much fun it is to paint and play and cook a crazy cake. Remember all messes, no matter how large, can be cleaned—and there is nothing wrong with getting your child to help! Most of all, remember you are equipping your child with the power of imagination. The kids and I have done hundreds of projects—all of them needing to be cleaned out, straightened up, and put away. I have one simple statement for my artists and inventors when it comes to buttoning up a project: "If you want me to help you with your mess, we need to do it now. If you want to wait to clean up, you are on your own." Then I stubbornly stick with their decision—even if it means they dawdle far too long on a ten-minute cleanup. Most of the time they want my help, and we work fast and hard together.

All of the projects in this book include a wet or gooey stage. I've sorted the messier (i.e., most fun) projects out for you. Each project with an icon like this: is best done outdoors or in a space where drips and mess are not a problem. Don't be noble. If it is a day where you don't feel like dealing with disorder, skip these activities and look for this icon: These projects are exceptionally easy and take little time or energy on your behalf to get rolling.

Mix it up. Do some messy projects. Do some neat ones. Then remind yourself that all great art and food and science begin with one simple word: Yes. Yes, it sounds fun. Yes, it can be done. Yes, now is the time.

Then do it.

Mighty Mold Garden

This project is the most effective way I know to demonstrate the need to wash our hands! We grew molds from the iguana's cage, from outside, and from under our fingernails. Use your imagination when collecting potential molds for your garden.

CONTROL

What you will need:

    5 baby food jars with lids

    2 cups hot water

    1 packet unflavored gelatin

    cotton string

magnified 2.5 × 10⁹

Zygomycetes
(bread mold)

yes Penicillium is what makes Penicillin

plasmodial slime mold

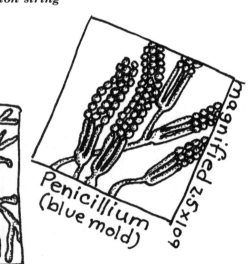

Penicillium
(blue mold)

magnified 2.5 × 10⁹

Lotions, Potions, and Slime

Sterilize the baby food jars with hot soapy water before beginning this project. Rinse, and pour boiling water into each jar and let it stand for a few minutes. Drain the water from the jars and allow to air dry. Boil the lids in water for 5 minutes. Sterilizing the jars ensures that your molds came from the collected bacteria and not from the jar itself.

Mix the gelatin into the 2 cups hot water and stir until dissolved. Gelatin is a good medium for growing molds because of its high protein content. Half fill the jars with the gelatin solution (you should have some gelatin solution left over). Place a lid on one of the jars. Write "Control" on masking tape and place it on the jar. A control will allow you to observe the changes in your other jars against the sterilized jar (where we will assume no bacteria can grow).

Cut 5 pieces of string around 8" long each. Dip the string into the leftover gelatin solution, and drag each piece around in different areas of the house. Consider collecting bacteria from your toes, mouth, fingernails, or your pet. Label each jar with the place you have collected from, and place the string into the gelatin solution. Place a lid on each jar. Write down a hypothesis (an educated guess) of which places will grow molds more quickly.

Now wait. Within a week (sometimes as fast as 24 hours) you should have a variety of molds growing in the solutions. Are they different? What happens to the gelatin when the molds take over? Which place grows mold the fastest? The slowest? Does that fit with your hypothesis?

Charcoal Crystal Garden

I remember this project when I was a girl, and it still hasn't lost its charm. A charcoal garden makes a good science fair project.

What you will need:

- *6 or 7 charcoal briquettes*
- *6 tablespoons warm water*
- *6 tablespoons liquid bluing (available at your grocer in the laundry section)*
- *4 tablespoons table salt*
- *1 tablespoon ammonia*

Pile the briquettes in a shallow dish. In a separate dish, mix the water and bluing together, then stir in the salt and the ammonia. Pour evenly over the charcoal.

What happens? Fluffy white crystals begin to grow on the charcoal. As the water in the solution evaporates, the chemicals left behind on the charcoal form crystals. These crystals are porous and the solution continues to be wicked up through them—resulting in layers of beautiful white crystals. For different crystal colors, place a few drops of food coloring onto the coals after pouring the solution. You can keep your garden growing by adding more solution every day.

Lotions, Potions, and Slime

Ice Bubbles

If you live in a temperate climate, try this when you find yourself in the middle of winter in the middle of the mountains, with nothing to do.

What you will need:

> *bubble solution*
>
> *bubble blower*

Choose a windless day below 32 degrees to do this project. Go outdoors and gently blow a bubble without releasing it. Keep the bubble on the blower, and you should be able to see ice crystals forming until the bubble freezes completely into a clear bubble of ice. Of course, the colder it is outside, the faster the bubble freezes!

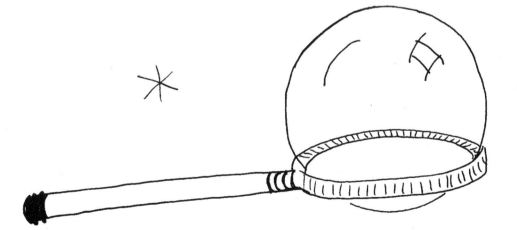

Green Pennies

Do this project before your child goes to sleep, and wake up to science in action!

What you will need:

paper towel

bowl

vinegar

pennies

Fold the paper towel into a square and lay it in the bowl. Pour enough vinegar onto the paper towel to saturate it. Lay the pennies on the wet paper towel. Wait until the next morning.

What happens? Overnight the underside of the pennies have grown a bright green coating. The copper in the pennies reacts with the vinegar to form a green substance called copper acetate. Green copper is also called verdigris. There are people who pay large amounts of money for verdigris ornaments and art!

Coat a Nail with Copper

Another wondrous project with pennies and vinegar. It takes only a few moments to put the ingredients together, although the project requires twenty-four hours to set.

What you will need:

20 pennies

1 clear plastic disposable cup

vinegar

1 heaping tablespoon salt

1 steel nail (not galvanized)

paper towel

Names of these elements:
C - Carbon   H - Hydrogen
Cl - chlorine   Na - Sodium
Cu - Copper   O - Oxygen
Fe - Iron

Place the 20 pennies in a cup. Next fill the cup with vinegar. Stir salt into the vinegar. Watch! What is happening to the pennies? Twist the nail tightly into a small piece of paper towel and drop it into the cup with the pennies. Leave the nail in the solution for 24 hours.

What happens? The nail will be covered with a shiny coat of copper. Molecules of copper from the pennies will have mixed into the solution and coated the nail's surface. The paper towel is the wick that brings the copper and salt solution to the nail's surface.

Experiment! What happens if you soak a nail without twisting it in the paper towel? Try 10 pennies per nail. Try 30 pennies per nail.

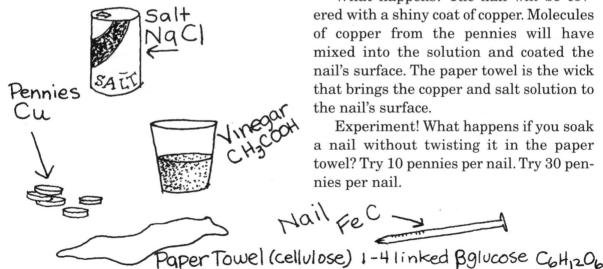

Salt NaCl

Pennies Cu

Vinegar CH_3COOH

Nail Fe C

Paper Towel (cellulose) 1-4 linked β glucose $C_6H_{12}O_6$

Marbled Milk

Even after doing this project dozens of times, each time feels fresh while we watch the amazing results! Be prepared to do this one over and over.

What you will need:

2% fat milk

small saucer

food coloring (in the squeeze bottles, several different colors)

liquid dish soap

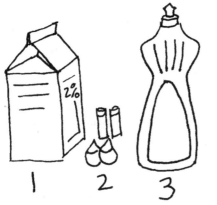

1   2   3

Pour the milk into the saucer to cover the bottom. Place 5 to 7 drops of different colored food coloring onto the milk. Next place one drop of the liquid detergent in the middle of the mixture. Incredible, isn't it?

What happens? When you add the detergent, the drops of food coloring twirl madly in swirly patterns across the surface of the milk. Why? The drops of food coloring first held together on the surface of the milk because of the fat molecules in the milk (water and oil don't mix, remember?). Adding the detergent to the milk breaks up the fat molecules and allows the food coloring to spread across the milk. What happens if you use 1% fat milk? Whole milk?

Grow Ice in a Straw

This is a vivid demonstration of how water expands when it turns to ice. You may have to try this one a couple of times to get it to work properly. But don't let that stop you—it is well worth the effort.

What you will need:

water

several straws

small piece of modelling clay

Run water through the straws, then plug one end of each with a bit of the clay. Fill the straws with water. Plug the tops with more clay. The trick to this project is to completely fill the straws with water. Be sure that there is no air space left in the straws and that there are no leaks from the clay caps. Lay the straws in the freezer.

What happens? When water inside the straw freezes, it expands and the tube of ice dramatically shoves the clay plug out.

BEFORE

AFTER

Boil Water in a Paper Cup

This trick is one of our favorite campfire activities.

What you will need:

campfire

paper cup filled with water

When the fire dies down, carefully place a paper cup of water onto the embers. In a few moments the water will begin to boil—without burning the cup!

How? Water boils at 212 degrees. Paper burns at over 450 degrees. The water keeps the paper below the temperature required to ignite it.

Lotions, Potions, and Slime

Water Maker

Ships at sea and de-salinization plants have water makers that transform salt water to fresh water with a process similar to this one.

What you will need:

  2 cups water

  pan with lid

  2 teaspoons salt

  oven mitts

LIFT THE LID AWAY FROM YOUR FACE. HOT!

Pour the water into the pan and stir in the salt. Have your child taste it. Yech! Salty, isn't it? Let's pretend this is the sea water your ship is going to make fresh water from. Bring the salty water to a boil and put the lid on. Simmer gently. Every few minutes remove the lid (are you wearing your oven mitts?) and tip the condensed steam that has collected on the lid into a bowl or glass. Do this several times until you have enough water to taste.

What happens? The salt minerals in the water were too heavy to collect on the lid as a vapor, so much of the salt remains in the pot (taste the salt water again after you remove it from the heat and it has cooled). The vapors that cool on the lid taste very close to fresh water.

Oobleck

Is it a liquid? A solid? Your child's imagination will blossom with Oobleck—a wondrous substance that uncovers all kinds of possibilities.

What you will need:
1 box (1 lb) cornstarch

1¹/₂ cups cold water

1 tablespoon food coloring

plastic dish pan or big bowl

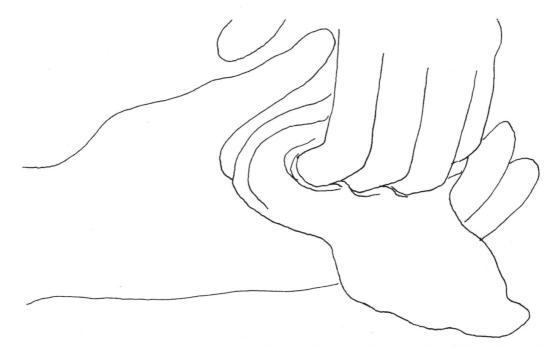

Mix the cornstarch, water, and food coloring in the container with your hands until it is smooth. Try this: Squeeze the Oobleck in your fist. Now open up your hand. Draw a finger down the center of the solution. Pound on the Oobleck, then feel it gently with your palm.

What happens? If you touch Oobleck gently, it is soft and yielding like liquid. When you squeeze it or pound it quickly, it is hard and crumbly. Why? Cornstarch is ground up into such fine particles that the molecules line up like little plates. When you pound the Oobleck, the cornstarch plates are rigid. When you move it slowly, the plates slide around and then act like a liquid.

This recipe makes enough Oobleck for several children to play with. You can make smaller amounts by mixing 2 parts cornstarch to 1 part water in a bowl. Oobleck will keep for several days if you continue to add water as it dries. Store in a covered container.

Silly Slime 🖐

This project is one of those exhilarating activities that everybody loves. By making and playing with this weird substance your child is exploring the scientific properties of an *elasto-viscous material.*

The earth is an example of an elasto-viscous material. When the earth is moved slowly, as in glacial movement or continental drift, the earth behaves like a liquid. When moved quickly or abruptly, as in an earthquake, the earth behaves like a solid and fractures. Silly Slime moves and stretches and fractures and slides in a most amazing way. And parents note: Buying the Borax and Elmer's glue is the hard part. This stuff is simple to make and easily cleaned up with a little water.

What you will need:

1 quart of water

¹/₄ cup Borax (Borax is available at your grocer in the laundry detergent section)

2 large jars with lids

1 cup Elmer's glue

1 cup water

food coloring

paper cups

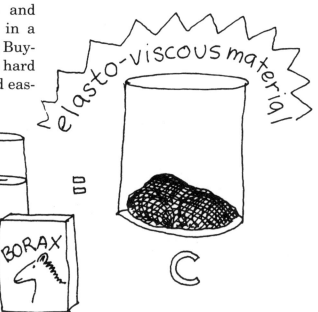

The ingredients for this recipe will make more Silly Slime than you might think you need, which is fine. Kids inevitably want to make more to show friends or to give away.

Place the 1 quart water and the Borax in one of the large jars. Stir to dissolve. Then pour the glue, the 1 cup water, and a few drops of food coloring together in the other jar, replace the lid, and shake hard. You now have 2 jars of solution: a Borax solution and a glue solution. To make the Silly Slime, pour 2 tablespoons of Borax solution into a paper cup. Stir in 6 table-spoons of glue solution. Watch! The mixture suddenly becomes thick and slimy. Stir hard, then pour off any extra liquid. Knead the Silly Slime with your hands until smooth.

Any 3-to-1 measure of glue solution to Borax solution will create Silly Slime (the glue contains polyvinyl acetate, which reacts with Borax). For example, 1 tablespoon Borax solution and 3 tablespoons glue solution will make a smaller quantity, while 1/3 cup Borax solution to 1 cup glue solution will make a huge amount! Silly Slime will also act like Silly Putty and copy newsprint when laid over the paper and pressed down firmly (comics are fun!). Store in a zipper-top plastic bag.

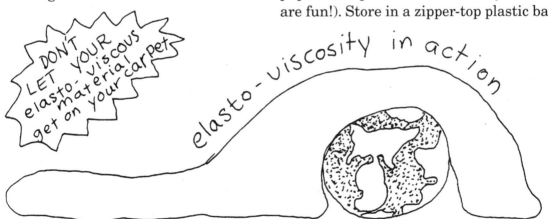

Travelling Toothpicks 🖐

If you don't have sugar lumps, try substituting several big spoonfuls of granulated sugar. The effect is the same, but the toothpicks are not quite as responsive as they are to the sugar lumps.

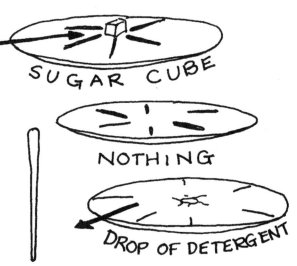

SUGAR CUBE

NOTHING

DROP OF DETERGENT

What you will need:

water

dinner plate

7 or 8 toothpicks

2 or 3 lumps of sugar

few drops of liquid detergent

Pour just enough water into the plate to float the toothpicks. When the water is still, lay the toothpicks with one end facing the center of the plate and the other end toward the rim. When you are finished, the toothpicks should be in a rough star shape with an empty circle in the center. Place the lumps of sugar in that center, one on top of the other. Watch carefully! Remove the sugar. Now place a few drops of the detergent into the center of the toothpick star.

What happens? When you place the sugar into the water, the toothpicks gravitate toward it. Why? The sugar absorbs water and pulls a small current of water toward itself, dragging the toothpicks along in the current. When you place the liquid detergent into the water, the toothpicks move away sharp and fast to the outside edges of the plate. Water has a "skin" caused by surface tension. The soap weakens this skin and the toothpicks are pulled by the stronger surface tension around the rim of the plate.

Lotions, Potions, and Slime

Density Discovery

This is a sinker/floater project for big kids. The more you experiment with different objects in the liquids, the greater will be your understanding of density.

ISOPROPYL A.

What you will need:

2 widemouthed jars or glasses

water

isopropyl alcohol (rubbing alcohol)

2 pieces of candle

H_2O

Fill one jar half full with water, the other with alcohol. Ask your child if she believes the candle will float or sink in each of the solutions. Then place a piece of candle in each jar.

What happens? The candle floats in the water and sinks in the alcohol. Why? An object in liquid will float or sink depending on how its density compares to that of the liquid. Water has a density of 1. Isopropyl alcohol has a density of around .76; wax, .85. Any item whose density is between 1 (water) and .76 (alcohol) will work effectively for this project. Experiment! Try an egg, a frozen pea, a plastic bead, a piece of crayon, rice, or a plastic Lego block.

Density Rainbow

Don't skip this project. It is a fascinating visual interpretation of the principle of density. I guarantee your whole family will be entranced.

What you will need:

corn syrup

measuring cup

food coloring (4 different colors)

tall glass

glycerine (available at your pharmacy)

spoon

water

olive oil

rubbing alcohol

You will be layering colored fluids that rest upon each other because of differing density. The secret to this project is to pour the fluids carefully enough not to disturb the previous layer. You begin with the heaviest fluid of the group, corn syrup, and end with the lightest fluid, rubbing alcohol.

ALCOHOL

H_2O

OLIVE OIL

GLYCERINE

CORN SYRUP

MAKE SURE THAT THE SPOON DOESN'T TOUCH THE TOP OF THE PREVIOUS LAYER

Ready? Pour an inch or two of corn syrup into a measuring cup, add a few drops of food coloring and stir. Pour it into the glass. Rinse the measuring cup and pour an inch or two of glycerine into the measuring cup. Add a few drops of another color of food coloring to the glycerine and stir. Use the spoon to place the glycerine on top of the syrup by holding the spoon in the glass (without touching the syrup) and pouring the glycerine gently onto the spoon. This helps to diffuse the fluid more gently than pouring the glycerine directly onto the syrup. Rinse the measuring cup and color an inch or two of tap water. Place the water onto the glycerine layer with the spoon as before. Pour some oil into the measuring cup and add it onto the water layer with the spoon (food coloring will not mix with oil, leave it natural). Your final layer is rubbing alcohol. Color it a different color in the measuring cup and add it to the glass with the spoon.

You now have five bright layers of different fluids. Here's the fun part: drop different small items into the glass and watch which layer they land in. You will be able to determine that different objects have different densities in relation to the fluids. As in the previous recipe, try rice, plastic beads, a small piece of wax, seeds, pencil lead, small pieces of Lego, a cork, or a grape. Experiment!

Homemade Icebergs

Discover why icebergs are so invisibly dangerous to boats. Make a few of these for the bathtub. Supply a few toy boats and demonstrate what happened to the Titanic.

What you will need:

plastic bags with twist ties (try different sizes for this project)

water

Fill the bags two-thirds full of water. Twist the ties on and place the bags in the freezer. When completely frozen, remove the icebergs from the plastic bags and measure each one from top to bottom. Estimate how much of the iceberg will remain above the water when placed in the tub. Then place the icebergs one at a time into the tub or sink full of water. Help your child figure out the percentage of ice that appears above the water and the percentage below the water.

Underwater Volcano

I don't know about your kids, but mine will try any project with the word "volcano" in it.

What you will need:

- *rubber band*
- *a small and narrow glass jar (a clean and empty spice jar works great)*
- *string*
- *a large glass jar (the bigger the better! We used a gallon jar, but a large peanut butter or pickle jar works, too.)*
- *cold water*
- *hot water*
- *few drops of red food coloring*

Place the rubber band snugly around the neck of the small jar. Tie the ends of the string onto the rubber band to make a handle. Fill the large jar with cold water. Fill the small jar with hot water and add a few drops of the red food coloring. Carefully lower the small jar into the large jar by the handle.

What happens? The hot water rises in a spectacular cloud of red to the surface of the cold water. Why? Because hot water is lighter than cold water and rises to the top of the jar. As the hot water cools, the red cloud will disperse evenly into the water.

Old-Fashioned Volcano

Another volcano! Make it for a science project or for the sheer fun of it. This volcano can be used over and over again, making it a fine gift for any child in love with lava.

What you will need:

newspaper

plastic shopping bag

empty baby bottle

masking tape

disposable aluminum oven liner

1 cup white glue

1 cup water

6 pieces of brown tissue paper cut into strips

clear acrylic spray (available at the hardware store)

1 tablespoon liquid dish detergent

1 teaspoon red food coloring

1 tablespoon baking soda

¹/₃ cup vinegar

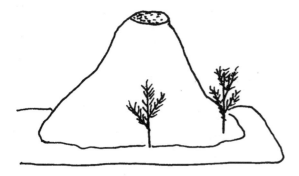

PLASTIC BAG

JAR FOR MOUTH OF VOLCANO

PAPER GOES INTO BAG

WITH PAPER INSIDE MAKE THE "MOUND"

Lotions, Potions, and Slime

To form the volcano, crumple up some of the newspaper and place into the plastic shopping bag. Nestle the baby bottle into the newspaper and gather the opening of the bag around the neck. Tape the bag into place around the neck of the bottle. Now reshape the volcano around the bottle (hint: use masking tape to help hold the volcano shape, spiraling the tape down from a rather narrow opening to a broader base). Place the bag on the oven liner.

Mix the glue and water together in a large bowl. Tear the remaining newspaper into strips. Begin by dipping the newspaper strips in the glue mixture. Make several layers of newspaper strips around the opening and down the volcano (allow the strips to run onto the oven liner). Lay several layers of the strips in a crisscross pat-

tern across and down the volcano. For the final layer, dip the tissue paper in the glue mixture and cover the volcano. Allow the volcano to dry for several days. When the volcano is dry, spray clear acrylic over it to seal.

Ready to try it out? Place the liquid detergent, food coloring, and baking soda into the bottle. Pour the vinegar in last. The vinegar (an acid) reacts with the baking soda (a base) to produce carbon dioxide. The pressure of the expanding carbon dioxide pushes the foam from the bottle, creating a spectacular lava effect! For a realistic setting, place small evergreen sprigs set in clay around the base of the volcano. When finished, carefully tip the volcano upside down in a sink to empty out the remainder of the lava.

PUT NEWSPAPER STRIPS OVER TOP

SPRAY CLEAR ACRYLIC

Cabbage Chemistry

Be sure to make up more dipsticks than you think you will need. Each time we do this project, we find new and wilder solutions to test—and experimenting is what science is all about!

What you will need:

a head of red cabbage

distilled water

$1/2$ lemon

cotton swabs

solutions to test the dip sticks in: ammonia, baking soda stirred into a little water, cream of tartar stirred into a little water, lemon juice, vinegar, orange juice, powdered cleanser stirred into a little water

P-H SCALE: ACIDS - RED

Cut the cabbage into small pieces and place into a pot. Add around 2 cups of distilled water and the juice from the lemon half (to help eliminate the aroma of cooking cabbage). Bring to a boil and simmer for 5 minutes. Remove from the heat. When the cabbage has cooled completely, drain the water from it into a large jar. Dip both ends of the cotton swabs into the solution and lay on a paper towel to dry. These are your dipstick indicators. When they are dry, you are ready to launch into the world of acids and bases.

Scientists use a scale called pH to measure the concentration of hydrogen ions in a particular substance. A pH of 7 is considered neutral (distilled water, for example). Anything above 7 is a base. Anything below 7 is an acid. Your dipsticks will determine if a substance is an acid or a base by reacting to the hydrogen in the substance. Acids will turn the dipstick red. Bases will turn the dipstick blue.

Prepare the solutions listed above and pour each in a small jar. Then dip a fresh dipstick into each testing solution to determine whether it is an acid or a base. Record your results.

A variation to the dipsticks is to place the cooled cabbage solution in several small jars and pour the testing solutions directly into the cabbage solution.

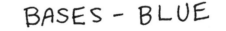

BASES - BLUE

Turmeric Dipsticks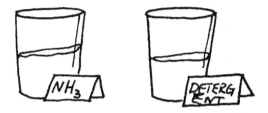

There is something utterly fascinating about this project. It is in the vivid colors, the magical way they change, and the powerful curiosity of your child drawn into the world of chemical reactions. Turmeric dipsticks are base indicators—a substance that turns another color in the presence of an acid or a base.

What you will need:

- *1/3 cup rubbing alcohol*
- *1/4 teaspoon turmeric (this spice may be available at your grocer, or check a specialty spice shop)*
- *cotton swabs*
- *solutions to test the dipsticks: ammonia, wood ashes dissolved in a little water, baking soda dissolved in a little water, lemon juice, vinegar, powdered cleanser dissolved in a little water, hand soap, glass cleaner*

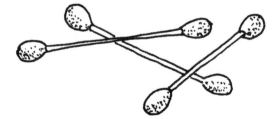

Pour the alcohol into a small jar and stir in the turmeric. Dip both ends of the cotton swabs into the turmeric solution and dry on a paper towel. First try the dipsticks with ammonia. Uncap a bottle of ammonia and hold the dipstick into the fumes that are escaping. Take care you do not breathe in the ammonia fumes.

What happens? The bright yellow dipstick turns abruptly and brilliantly red within seconds. The ammonia fumes are a base and turn the dipstick indicator red. Dip the red dipstick into vinegar. What happens? The dipstick turns yellow again. Vinegar is an acid, which cancels out, or neutralizes, the base ammonia and returns the dipstick to its former yellow color. Now try the dipsticks in the remaining solutions. Record your results.

Carbon Dioxide Balloons

Don't just blow up those balloons—fill them with carbon dioxide!

What you will need:

1 tablespoon baking soda twisted in a piece of toilet paper (this makes it easier to slip into the bottle)

empty soda bottle

1 cup vinegar

balloons

Place the baking soda twisted in toilet paper into the bottle. Add the vinegar and *quickly* place the balloon over the mouth of the bottle. Tie off the balloon after it has filled.

What happens? The baking soda and vinegar react to create carbon dioxide and the gas fills the balloon. Take this project one step further. Blow up a balloon slightly larger than the carbon dioxide balloon and tie it off. Hold both balloons out at arm's length and ask your child which will hit the ground first. You will both be very surprised!

Pop Your Top!

Most film developers have a stash of empty film cannisters they are willing to give away. Any type of plastic cannister will work, but a clear one offers a window to what is happening inside. Be safe! Make sure to wear eye protection while doing this experiment.

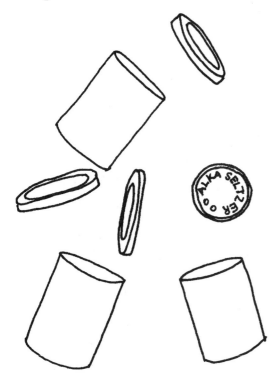

What you will need:
Alka-Seltzer tablets
glass half filled with water
a small bowl of water
plastic film cannisters with lids

Begin by dropping an alka-seltzer tablet into the glass half filled with water. As you and your child observe the fizz, talk about what is happening. Ask what he thinks will happen if you put a tablet and water in a film cannister with the lid on (this is your child's hypothesis).

Go outdoors with the bowl of water, the cannisters, and the Alka-Seltzer tablets. Drip 5 drops of water off the tip of your finger into the film cannister. Then place an Alka-Seltzer tablet into the film cannister and quickly replace the lid.

What happens? Within a few seconds the lid pops off and flies into the air. Alka-Seltzer creates carbon dioxide gas when combined with water. This gas quickly fills the container and the increasing pressure causes the lid to pop off. Experiment! What happens if you use half a tablet? Increase the amount of water? Decrease the amount of water?

Lotions, Potions, and Slime

Rubber Egg

Change a hard smooth egg into a thing my family imagines baby dinosaurs could spring from.

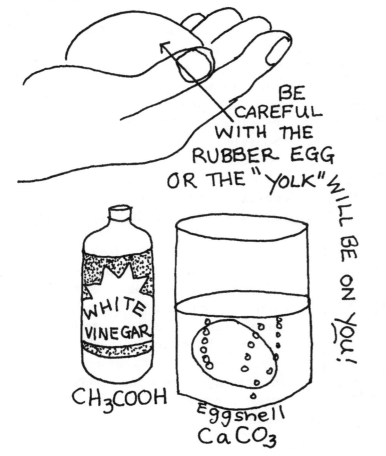

BE CAREFUL WITH THE RUBBER EGG OR THE "YOLK" WILL BE ON YOU!

CH₃COOH

Eggshell CaCO₃

What you will need:
egg

small glass jar

vinegar

Place the egg in the jar and cover with vinegar. Soon tiny bubbles will cover the shell.

What happens? Over the next several hours the hard shell of the egg disappears, leaving the flexible and rubbery egg sac that surrounds the white and yolk intact. The vinegar is an acid that dissolves the calcium in the shell.

One-Fisted Egg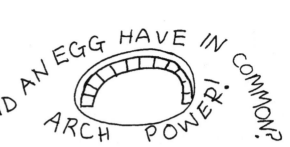

This is an old trick that continues to charm and fascinate kids of all ages.

What you will need:

1 raw egg

1 rubber glove

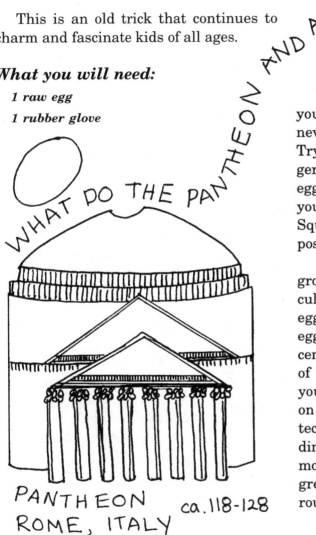

WHAT DO THE PANTHEON AND AN EGG HAVE IN COMMON? ARCH POWER!

PANTHEON ROME, ITALY ca. 118-128

No matter how strong you are, how young or old you are, you will probably never be able to crush an egg in your fist. Try it. Remove any rings from your fingers, put on a rubber glove, and place an egg in the palm of your hand. Now wrap your fingers around the egg and squeeze. Squeeze harder. Squeeze as hard as you possibly can.

What happens? Nothing. Even a full-grown, muscular hand will have a difficult, if not impossible, time cracking the egg. Why? When you normally crack an egg, you tap it on the edge of a bowl, concentrating the force upon one small area of the egg. When you squeeze an egg in your fist, you are applying equal pressure on all sides of one of the strongest architectural shapes in the world—the three-dimensional arch. If your egg breaks, it is most likely because one finger has applied greater pressure to the shell than surrounding fingers.

Lotions, Potions, and Slime

Jumpin' Gelatin

An element of surprise enhances this project.

What you will need:
1 package flavored gelatin
1 package unflavored gelatin
balloon

Pour half of the package of flavored gelatin granules onto a small saucer. Pour the whole package of the unflavored gelatin onto another small saucer. Blow up the balloon and tie it off. Rub the balloon on your head until your hair is full of static (a piece of wool works too). Hold the static side of the balloon over the flavored gelatin. Watch and listen. Brush the balloon off into the sink, and rub on your hair once again. Hold over the unflavored gelatin granules.

What happens? Rubbing the balloon on your hair transfers extra electrons to the balloon. These extra electrons make a static charge and attract the protein fibers in the gelatin. The movement is particularly dramatic in the unflavored gelatin, forming columns of gelatin several inches long!

Electric Jell-O Gumdrops

Take the last experiment one step further and explore the strange idea of a liquid suspended in a solid.

What you will need:

flavored gelatin

eye dropper (I buy mine at the local university bookstore in the science supplies section—or you can empty and rinse containers from small food coloring squeeze bottles, or drip from the tip of your finger)

glass of water

Pour the gelatin into a small dish if you haven't already. Begin by squeezing or dripping one drop of water onto the pile of gelatin. Watch how the water is absorbed and disappears. Slowly add another ten drops to the same spot, waiting for each drop to be absorbed before adding another. Scoop the pile up with a fork and lift it: a gumdrop!

What happens? The gelatin, combined with the sugar and flavoring, swells and holds the water with a net of protein fibers. Look closely. This gumdrop is actually a liquid within a solid. Experiment! Try making a gumdrop with the unflavored gelatin, or with a package of Kool-Aid. What happens?

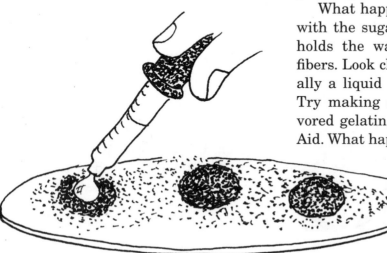

Lotions, Potions, and Slime

Fossil Fun

This is an effective way to demonstrate how real fossils are made. Do this project for the next science fair.

What you will need:

enough modelling clay to cover the bottom of a shoe box around 2 inches deep

shoe box

tiny plastic dinosaurs or creatures, weeds, seashells, thick-veined leaves, etc.

plaster of paris (available at your hardware store)

dark brown shoe polish (the waxy kind, not liquid)

Press 2 inches of modelling clay into the bottom of the box. This is the "mud" that helped preserve the shape of plant and animal debris millions of years ago. Press the fossil items into the clay (rub the leaves and plants into the clay with your finger) and pull them out, leaving the imprint of the item in the clay.

Mix the plaster of paris according to the directions on the box (or add water to the plaster until it is the consistency of pancake batter) and pour over the imprinted clay to a depth of around 1½ to 2 inches thick. Explain that the plaster is similar to the lava or mud that hardened over real plants and shells. Let the plaster firm up overnight in a warm place, then peel the box and modelling clay away from the plaster and lift from the clay. Rub the shoe polish over the plaster fossils with a soft rag to highlight them.

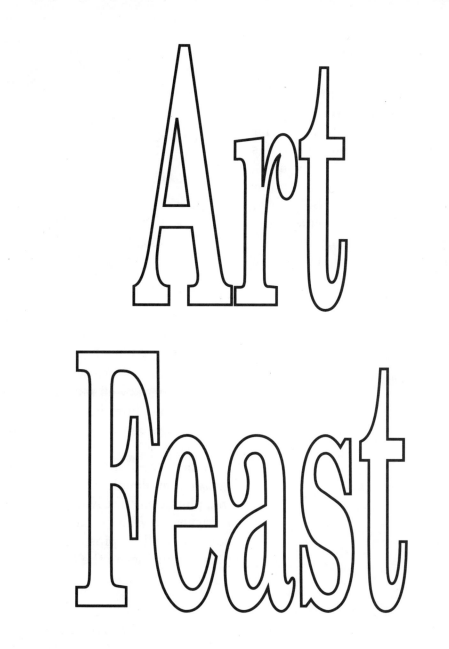

Glitter Play-Dough

Through four children and twelve years, play-dough is still a favorite around our home. This recipe is infinitely superior to the store-bought stuff, and two things make it special: the icing food coloring paste (it makes a deeper color that regular food coloring cannot match—available at your grocer or specialty-food shop) and glitter. Or choose to keep it simple and use ordinary food coloring and skip the glitter.

What you will need:

3 cups flour

1¹/₂ cups salt

**6 teaspoons cream of tartar
   (acts as a preservative)**

3 cups water

3–4 tablespoons oil

icing food coloring

glitter

Mix the dry ingredients (except the glitter) together in a big pan. Add the water, oil, and food coloring, and whisk until the lumps are worked out and the food coloring is well mixed. Place the mixture over medium heat and stir until the dough thickens and gathers into a big ball.

When the dough cools, knead in the glitter. Play-dough will keep several weeks in a plastic bag or covered bowl (no need to refrigerate). When ready to use, add cookie cutters, rolling pins, table knives, and plastic figurines to the fun.

ABC Dough

The best way to learn the alphabet. Make it, bake it, hang it on a wall! This recipe makes enough dough to create the whole alphabet.

What you will need:

- *1 cup salt*
- *1½ cups hot water*
- *3½–4 cups white flour*
- *26 small pieces of wire to make hangers*
- *puffy paints*
- *paintbrush*

Preheat oven to 300 degrees. Pour the salt into a medium-sized bowl and add the hot water. Stir until the salt partly dissolves (it will not dissolve completely). Allow to cool, and then add 1 cup of flour and mix until all the lumps are worked out. Add another cup of flour and stir. The next 1½ cups of flour need to be squeezed into the dough by hand. If the dough seems a little sticky, add a bit more flour; too dry, add a few drops of water. Knead the dough until smooth and pliable.

You are ready to make the alphabet. Pinch off a large walnut-sized piece of clay and roll into a snake. Form the letter *A*. Continue to make the letters of the alphabet out of walnut-sized pieces of clay. Don't try to make all the letters perfectly uniform. You can buy alphabets that look perfect—this one should express your and your child's imagination! Lay the letters on a lightly greased cookie sheet and press a small piece of wire into the top of each for a hanger. To improve the texture and join pieces in a letter, wet your finger in water and run it over the clay until smooth.

Bake the letters for 30 minutes. When cool, the letters are ready to paint. Use the puffy paints to decorate the letters in wild colors and patterns.

Play Clay

The texture and color of this rich-looking clay makes it a stand out for kids. Use it like play dough or make a set of checkers or chess pieces.

What you will need:

 1 cup baking soda

 $^1/_2$ cup cornstarch

 tempera paint (for coloring the dough—
  tubes of water color, fabric dye, and
  food coloring also work well)

 $^3/_4$ cup cold water

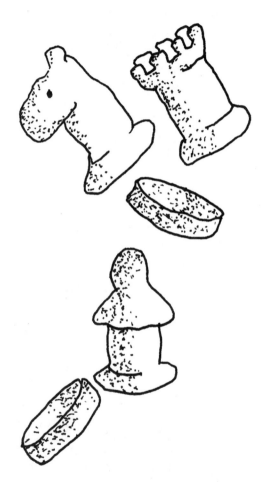

Have your child mix the baking soda and cornstarch together with her hands in a medium-sized saucepan. Add the paint to the cold water, stir until dissolved, and pour into the saucepan. Set the pan on the stove over medium heat, and stir constantly just until the mixture gathers together (if you overcook this dough, it will be too crumbly to work with). When the dough cools, knead it until smooth and pliable. This clay will keep in a covered container for a week.

Lotions, Potions, and Slime

Sparkle Salt Dough

This is a creative clay with flash. Try making several batches in different colors.

What you will need:

³/₄ cup cold water

1 tablespoon food coloring

1 cup salt

¹/₂ cup cornstarch

Pour the water and food coloring into a medium-sized pan. Stir in the salt and cornstarch. Cook over medium heat, stirring constantly until the mixture thickens and gathers together. Take the lump of dough out and wrap in a paper towel. When it is cool, knead for a few minutes. This dough keeps well in a plastic bag in the refrigerator.

Desi's Edible Dough

Desi is an imaginary friend who loves to eat. What could be more fun than modelling dough you can eat? Desi's Edible Dough makes a healthy snack, too!

What you will need:
1 cup peanut butter
1 cup honey
2¹/₃ cups powdered milk
large bowl

Place all the ingredients in the bowl and have your child squeeze everything together with his hands until thoroughly mixed. (The texture of the dough is improved if you place the powdered milk in a blender and blend it to a fine powder, but this is an optional step.) If, after mixing, the dough is too sticky, add a little more powdered milk. Too dry, add more peanut butter. Play with the dough as you would any modelling dough: make pancakes, snowmen, teddy bears, hearts, and stars. Use raisins or currants to decorate the creations. Then eat!

Lotions, Potions, and Slime

Crepe Paper Clay: Holiday Votives

Who can resist the magic of a meal eaten by candlelight? These votives are made with a special clay that sticks to glass. Kids can use their imagination and sculpt the clay into a three-dimensional object around the jar, or cut out stars or holiday shapes to let the candlelight glow through.

What you will need:

1 cup crepe paper clippings (tear or cut crepe paper into fine pieces, pack them into the cup somewhat firmly)

1 cup warm water

$^1/_2$–$^2/_3$ cup white flour

3 clean baby food jars with the labels off

3 votive candles

Place the clippings into a bowl and cover with the warm water. Let the mixture set for several hours until the crepe paper is smooth and pliable (you can do this overnight). The water breaks down the crepe paper fibers and makes an extraordinary clay when flour is added.

Pour off all the water, and stir $^1/_2$ cup of flour into the crepe paper. If it seems too sticky, add the remaining flour. Knead the dough on a floured countertop, adding flour as needed until the clay reaches the consistency of pie crust dough. Divide into 3 pieces, and roll or flatten the clay into a longish rectangle that will circle the jar. Press the clay onto the jar and smooth the seam with your fingers. Use a butter knife (fingers work too in this soft clay) to cut holiday shapes out around the jar for letting the light peek through (simple squares and circles also look great). Put one votive candle in each jar. My sons listened to none of these instructions and immediately created wonderful faces on the jars with big noses and bushy eyebrows. So my advice to you: Let those imaginations go!

Permanent Sand Castle

On your next visit to the beach, bring home a bag of sand and make sand sculptures that tides and time won't touch! (Sand can also be purchased at the hardware store or building supply store.) Make a small sand castle using tiny cups and boxes as forms, or triple the recipe for a king-size castle.

What you will need:

2 cups sand

1/3 cup wheat paste powder (available at your hardware store)

1 cup water

Mix the sand and wheat paste powder with your hands in a large bowl. Add the water and stir everything up until it has the consistency of clay. Bring out the cookie cutters, paper cups, cans, spoons, forks, and knives to sculpt this clay into fabulous creations. Use a piece of plywood or cardboard as a base if you are making a sand castle. This clay may take several days to dry.

Lotions, Potions, and Slime

Soapy Dough

This is an easy uncooked dough you can make in minutes. Make several batches in different colors and use for modeling.

What you will need:

- *¼ cup salt*
- *1 cup flour*
- *1 tablespoon liquid tempera paint*
- *¼ cup water*
- *1 tablespoon liquid dish soap*

Place the salt and flour in a bowl and stir together. Add the paint, water, and dish soap and squeeze the mixture in your hands until everything is incorporated. If the dough seems too dry, add a little water. This dough works well with cookie cutters. Provide a variety of them along with a rolling pin. Seal the dough in a plastic bag when finished and refrigerate.

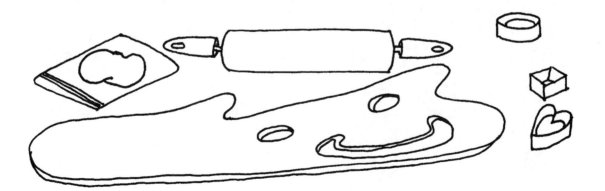

Finger Paint

Painting projects are not often a parent's first choice for their child to creatively express herself. But your child will be thrilled with the opportunity to experiment with these weird and wonderful paint recipes. And trust me—the few minutes of cleanup will be well worth the hands-on happiness of your child.

Finger paint sounds messy, but with a little supervision, it is a surprisingly easy project—and a splendid way to spend time. Finger paint also makes a great gift.

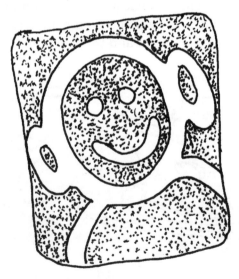

What you will need:

¹/₂ cup cornstarch

³/₄ cup cold water

2 cups hot water

1 tablespoon glycerine (this helps the consistency of the paint, and slows the drying process—available at your pharmacy)

tempera paints

Place the cornstarch in a pot and add half the cold water. Stir until it is smooth. Next whisk in the hot water and work out all the lumps. Cook the mixture over medium-low heat, stirring constantly, until it begins to boil. Remove from heat and stir in the glycerine and the remainder of the cold water. When the mixture has cooled slightly, divide into small jars and add a squirt of paint to color. Stir the paint and cornstarch mixture together until it is thoroughly mixed. Use the finger paint on any type of paper. I prefer poster paper to cover the entire table (tape it into place) for a hands-on marathon!

Lotions, Potions, and Slime

Finger Lickin' Finger Paints

Is your child tired of the same old finger paint experience? Here are two edible finger paints he will love. Do these projects outside on a nice day.

Finger Paint in a Can

What you will need:
1 can whipping cream
food coloring
finger paint paper or butcher paper

Tape the finger paint paper or the butcher paper, glossy side up, onto a table. Shake up the can of whipping cream and hand it over to your child. Have him spray the paper randomly with the cream and add a few drops of food coloring. Use fingers and hands (and toes?) to create the tastiest design ever!

Gelatin Finger Paint

What you will need:

finger paint paper or butcher paper

spray bottle filled with water

1 small box fruit-flavored gelatin

Tape the paper to a table. Spray water onto the paper and sprinkle the dry gelatin onto the paper. Begin to paint! Spray more water onto the paper as the gelatin absorbs it. This is an incredibly tactile project that moves your child through the sensory experiences of dry and gritty to slimy and then to sticky.

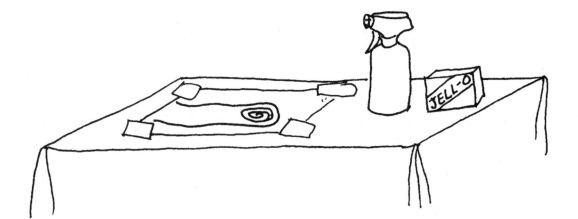

Feel-Good Foot Paint

Who says finger paint can't become foot paint? This paint feels positively luscious between your toes. Make up several colors and join your kids—create a one-of-a-kind painting no one will forget.

What you will need:

- *½ cup dry laundry starch (available in the laundry section of most grocery stores)*
- *2 cups cold water*
- *½ cup mild detergent soap flakes (grate a bar of soap if soap flakes aren't available)*
- *1 tablespoon tempera paint*
- *long piece of butcher paper (ask the people in the meat department of your grocer for a long piece)*

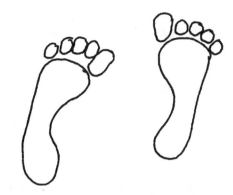

Stir the laundry starch and the cold water together. Cook over medium heat, stirring constantly, until the mixture is thick and glossy. Remove from the heat and whisk in the soap flakes and paint. When the paint is cool, it is ready to use.

Tape the butcher paper onto the sidewalk or driveway. Place the paint in large pans (9-by-13-inch pans work great) and set the pans near the paper. Take off your shoes and either sponge the paint onto the soles of your feet, or step into the paint and onto the paper.

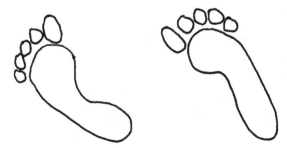

Spangled Salt Paint

This paint has a beautiful texture, adding a dimension of glitz and sparkle to your child's artwork. Try painting an underwater fish scene.

What you will need:

1 teaspoon liquid starch (available in the laundry section of your grocer)

1 teaspoon water

$\frac{1}{2}$ teaspoon liquid tempera paint

2 teaspoons table salt

Mix the starch, water, and paint together in a saucer. Stir in the salt and get out the brushes!

Impasto

Looking for a new experience with paint? Impasto is a thick layer of paint that you design into—like finger paint without using your fingers.

What you will need:

- *¹/₄ cup liquid tempera paint*
- *¹/₄ cup powdered laundry starch (you can also use liquid starch, but the paint will be thinner—both are available in the detergent section of your grocer)*
- *construction paper*
- *items to press through the paint: combs, cotton swabs, paintbrush (use both ends), jar lids, pencil, etc.*

Whisk the paint and starch together until well mixed. It should be as thick as frosting if you are using the powdered starch. Select a contrasting color of construction paper and spread the paint completely over the paper with a paintbrush (or wedge the paint on in designs with a narrow paint scraper). While the paint is still wet, run through it with the items (like you do with your fingers in finger painting).

Sidewalk Paint

My favorite projects in the whole world are those that send kids outdoors, armed with color and imagination and energy. Participate in the mural making if you want. Or simply watch the pure pleasure of a child releasing art onto the world. Sidewalk paint is nontoxic as well as biodegradable.

What you will need:

1 cup water

1 cup powdered nonfat milk

¼ teaspoon icing food coloring (available at most grocers)

paintbrushes in a variety of sizes

sponges

The icing food coloring is a paste instead of a liquid and will give you glorious colors of paint. However, you can also use regular food coloring in a pinch.

Pour the water in a jar. Add the milk and the food coloring and stir thoroughly until the paste is incorporated into the milk. You should have a vivid paint. Make up several colors. Supply your child with paintbrushes and sponges, and ask for a mural to decorate your driveway or sidewalk. At the end of the art project, the painting can be hosed off. Some residue of food coloring may remain, but it disappears with time and weather.

Sponge Mitt Painting

Finger painting for the fastidious! Provide a long sheet of butcher paper on a hot summer day and turn your budding Picasso loose.

What you will need:

butcher paper

several colors of tempera paint

sponge mitt (available at your grocer in the rubber glove section)

Lay out a long piece of the butcher paper. Pour the paint into saucers. Place the sponge mitt on your child's hand. He will dip into the tempera and paint away! Experiment. Suggest that he try placing different colors of paint onto the sponge mitt in different sections and rolling the mitt around the paper.

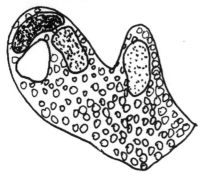

Bubble Prints

Make note cards and stationery with bubble prints. Plan ahead—these make nice gifts for the holiday season.

What you will need:

¹/₂ cup bubble solution

small plastic bowl

2 tablespoons tempera paint

straw

white typing paper cut in halves or quarters

Pour the bubble solution into the bowl. Whisk in the tempera paint. Use the straw to blow into the bubble solution and make a heap of bubbles. Lay a piece of paper gently over the bubbles. The paper will absorb the paint and make a print of your bubbles.

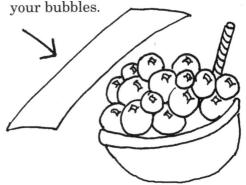

Tie-Dye Solution

Tie-dyeing tee shirts is an annual summertime event in our household. We save tee shirts all year—often picking them up for under a dollar at thrift shops or garage sales. Try tie-dying your handkerchiefs, socks, or pillowcases, too.

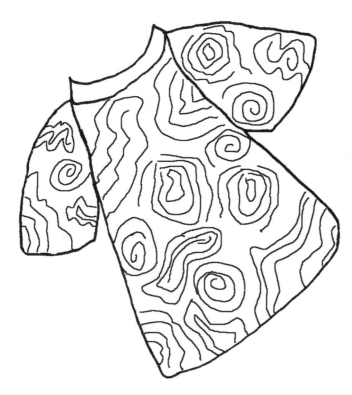

What you will need:

rubber gloves

2 packages each of powdered fabric dye in 3 or more different colors (doubling up on the dye gives deeper colors)

plastic bucket for each dye color

$1/2$ cup salt for each dye color

1 gallon of hot water for each dye color

plain white tee shirts (washed and dried)

rubber bands (a variety of sizes)

There are many types of dye, and many methods of tie-dyeing, but we have used this recipe for years with great success. Tie-dye outdoors, and you will keep this project free from mess or worry. Allow each individual her own dipping and dyeing method. Provide rubber gloves for those who don't want green fingers all day.

For each color, empty 2 packages of dye into a bucket, and add ½ cup of salt. Pour approximately a gallon of hot water into the dye/salt mixture. Stir the solution until everything is dissolved.

While you are mixing the dye, have the kids create patterns on the tee shirts by pulling up a piece of each shirt into a big cone and tightly placing rubber bands around the cone from top to bottom. Pull up several cones, or make one big starburst pattern in the middle of the shirt. Don't stop there! You can twist the cone, fold it into a fan and rubber band it down, or invent your own unique pattern! Small children may need help placing the rubber bands tightly.

When you are finished binding the cones into place with the rubber bands, dip the shirt (or a single cone) into the bucket of dye and hold for a few moments—the longer you keep it in the dye, the deeper the color. You can try a different color on each cone, or stick with a single color for the whole tee shirt. Gently wring out the excess dye and hang the tee shirts on a clothesline until dry (I have always loved the look of these dazzling shirts in a row—like national flags from the Republic of Self). Keep in mind the shirts may bleed the first few washings, and wash them separately in cold water (with 1 cup vinegar the first time).

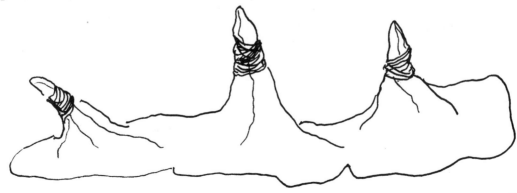

Kool-Aid Dye

If yours is a Kool-Aid kid, you know how the stuff stains things. Everything—shirts, pants, Sunday clothes. For years I struggled to wash and scrub and bleach the blotches out. Now here's your chance to put those colors to good use. Kool-Aid makes absolutely fabulous dyes in unusual colors for tee shirts, tissue paper (great gift wrap), wool, and eggs. Double this recipe if working with big batches of items to dye.

What you will need:

- **1 package Kool-Aid powdered drink mix**
- **¹⁄₄ cup vinegar**
- **2 cups water**

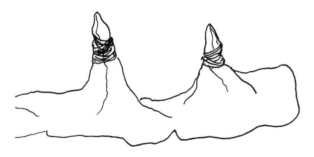

Stir the ingredients together in a pot. Bring the solution to a boil and remove from heat. If you are dyeing eggs, place the cooled dye in a jar and color the eggs as you would with ordinary egg dye.

To tie-dye tee shirts, pull up pieces of the shirt and tightly wrap rubber bands down the cone shape you have made. Wear rubber gloves. For deep colors, dip the bound cones of the shirt into the hot dye. Or do as I do and pour many colors of the cooled dye into buckets, go outside, and turn your kids loose with their rainbow ideas.

Rainbow Pasta

There are a multitude of interesting pasta shapes available today, and this recipe will turn them into a riot of colors. Whether you color macaroni or tiny rabbits, your child will find a dozen ways to use them. Glue them on paper and make cards, string them for necklaces, use them as game pieces, or, most fun of all, make clever pictures using colored damp spaghetti (it sticks to paper when damp, but it may not when dry, so use that glue). Remind kids—especially toddlers—not to eat the pasta.

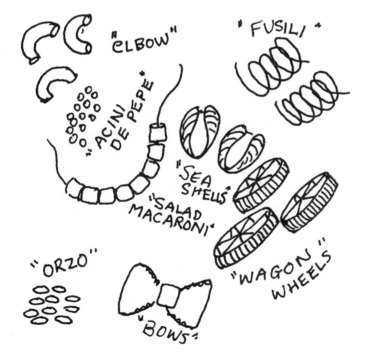

What you will need:

1¹/₂ cups rubbing alcohol

food coloring

1 cup dried pasta of your choice

Place the rubbing alcohol in a jar—for smaller pasta use a quart jar, spaghetti will need a longer container. Stir 3 teaspoons of food coloring into the alcohol, and add the pasta. Allow the pasta to soak in the dye for several hours. The pasta is ready when it reaches a deep, rich color. Drain the pasta (reserving the dye in a covered container for future pasta projects) and place in a single layer on paper towels. When the pasta is dry, it is ready to be used.

Cabbage Paper

Cabbage makes a translucent paper with a beautiful texture—truly a work of art! Save some of the cabbage pulp for Cabbage Paper II.

What you will need:

1 head of red or green cabbage cut into pieces

bucket

juice from 1 lemon

newspaper

several pieces of screen (available at your hardware store)

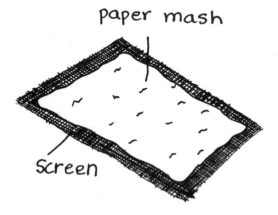

Soak the cabbage in a bucket of water for 2 days. Drain and place in a big pot along with the lemon juice (to help reduce the pungent odor of cooking cabbage). Add water and cook the cabbage until soft. Cool in the pot, then pour into a colander. Stir the cabbage pulp vigorously in the colander to drain excess water.

Place a pad of newspapers under each piece of screen. Spoon one heaping cup of the cabbage pulp onto the screen and, using a spoon, smooth the pulp out thinly on the screen. Be sure there are no bare spots in the pulp. Allow the paper to dry completely (around 1 to 2 days depending on the humidity of your environment). When dry, bend the screen out from under the cabbage paper and gently peel it off. You can make a book cover with it by applying an adhesive spray to a piece of cardboard. Press the cabbage paper onto the cardboard and trim.

Cabbage Paper II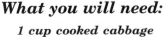

This paper is not as fragile or translucent as the first cabbage paper. You will be able to make sturdy pieces of paper to write on or use as a book cover for a handmade journal.

What you will need:

1 cup cooked cabbage pulp

1 cup toilet paper torn into tiny pieces

blender

1 tablespoon plaster of paris

newspaper

several pieces of screen (available at your hardware store)

Place the cabbage pulp and toilet paper in the blender. Fill with water and blend the mixture together. Next add the plaster of paris and blend together. Drain the slurry into a colander, stirring the excess water out.

Place a pad of newspapers under the pieces of screen. Then lay a cupful of the slurry onto the screen. Smooth it out thinly with the back of a spoon (be sure there are no bare spots). Dry for several days, then gently peel the paper from the screen.

WHAT I WOULD DO WITH A MILLION DOLLARS

MAKE A CABBAGE-PAPER BOOK

Homemade Glue

Does your family go through glue and paste like wild-fire? Here's an easy glue recipe that works well on paper materials.

What you will need:

- *2 cups cold water*
- *3 tablespoons cornstarch*
- *squeeze bottle (the type you buy for mustard and catsup)*

Pour the water into a medium-sized pot and stir in the cornstarch. Place over medium heat and stir constantly until the mixture is thick and clear. Remove from the heat. Pour into the squeeze container when cool.

Lotions, Potions, and Slime

Glue Art

Glue art makes wonderful cards, or you can peel it off wax paper and hang your creation in a mobile.

What you will need:

¹/₂ cup white glue

squeeze bottle (the type used for catsup)

1 tablespoon tempera paint

wax paper or construction paper

Pour glue into a squeeze bottle and add tempera paint. Shake it up or stir with a chopstick to mix the paint and glue thoroughly. Squeeze the colored glue onto a piece of wax paper (write a message, make stars and hearts, or just squiggle away), then let it dry and peel off the wax paper. To make unusual cards, draw or write with the colored glue on construction paper.

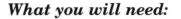

Lick and Stick

Make a stamp or a sticker (the kind you lick) out of any small drawing or pictures from a magazine.

What you will need:
- *2 tablespoons cold water*
- *1 packet plain gelatin*
- *3 tablespoons boiling water*
- *$1/2$ teaspoon corn syrup*
- *flavored extract such as orange, mint, or lemon*

Pour the cold water into a small bowl and sprinkle the package of gelatin over it. With a fork, whisk in the boiling water and stir until dissolved. Add the corn syrup and a few drops of extract (to make the stamp a tasty lick).

Have your child create a stamp or sticker or cut out small pictures from a magazine. With a finger or a paint brush apply a thin layer of the solution onto the back of the picture and let it dry. When ready, lick and stick!

This recipe will gel. To return to a liquid state for reuse, spoon into a jar and place the jar in a bowl of hot water.

Sidewalk Chalk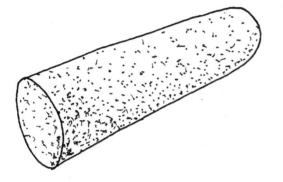

Turn that frustrated graffiti artist loose with this recipe for Sidewalk Chalk. It is brighter, darker, and more dramatic looking than ordinary chalk. You can also use it on paper for a tamer indoor chalk painting.

What you will need:

6 tablespoons sugar

2 cups warm water

sidewalk chalk (any type chalk will work)

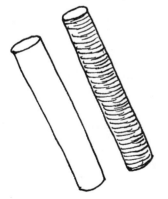

Stir the sugar into the warm water until dissolved. Place the chalk in a pan or bowl and pour the solution over it. Soak for several hours. Then drain the chalk, wipe off the excess moisture with a paper towel, and you are ready to roll! You can draw on paper or on the sidewalk. This soft chalk creates a wonderfully dense coat of color.

Helping-Hand Spoon Rest

Everyone needs a spoon rest beside the stove, and this one is as much fun to make as it is useful. Sculpey clay is used here because it is more pliable and easier to roll out than other clays on the market.

What you will need:

2 packages (2 different colors) of Sculpey clay

rolling pin

medium-sized oven-safe glass bowl

270° for 30 min

Preheat oven to 270 degrees. Break off several pieces of the clay and mash them together in your hands (using 2 colors gives your hand a marvelous marbled look). By twisting the clay together, or rolling it in your hands, you will incorporate the pieces into one bi-colored mass. Don't blend the colors completely.

Roll out the clay to the thickness of rolled cookies. Lay the palm of your hand on the clay and trace it with a knife to cut the spoon rest out. Lift gently from the clay with a spatula and lay the hand in the bowl. The curve of the bowl will curve the spoon rest nicely as it bakes. Bake for 30 minutes. Let cool and use.

Lotions, Potions, and Slime

BEFORE XEROX

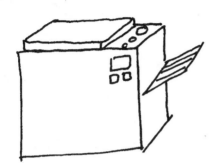

THERE WAS GEL

(THEY WERE CALLED "DITTOS")

Primitive Printer

A pair of my favorite four-year-olds came visiting when we were making a primitive printer, and these tiny experts deemed it a hit.

What you will need:
6 tablespoons very hot water

2 envelopes unflavored gelatin

1 teaspoon liquid dish soap

paper dinner plate

colored felt tip marker pens

Place the hot water in a glass measuring cup. Add the gelatin and stir until it is completely dissolved. Gently stir in the liquid dish soap, taking care not to create too many bubbles. Pour the mixture onto the paper plate. It should firm up within 15 minutes.

Draw a picture on the surface of the gelatin with the marker pens. Then lay a white piece of paper over the image and trace it with your fingers. Pull off the paper. Voila! A print! Use the printer while fresh for best results.

Bubble Tubes

I like to think of this as a project for all ages. Older kids love making bubble tubes, and younger siblings love playing with them.

What you will need:

2 feet of clear plastic tubing, 1 inch in diameter (available at your hardware store)

2 corks to fit the ends of the tubing

cool-melt glue gun

water

food coloring

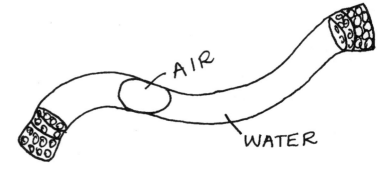

Take the plastic tubing and securely glue a cork into one end with the glue gun such that the cork won't come out. Fill the tube with water to within an inch of the uncorked end. Add a few drops of food coloring. Glue the other cork into the open end. Tip the tube back and forth and watch the bubble travel (toddlers love this). Experiment! Try oil with a few drops of colored water. Use glycerine instead of water and add glitter or small beads to the liquid. Be safe: always check to see that the corks are securely glued in place. Your child could make a bubble tube as a birthday gift for his favorite one-year-old!

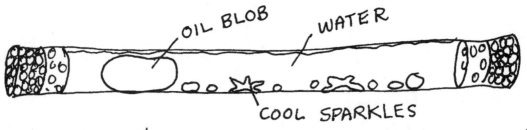

A CARPENTER'S LEVEL WORKS THE SAME WAY!

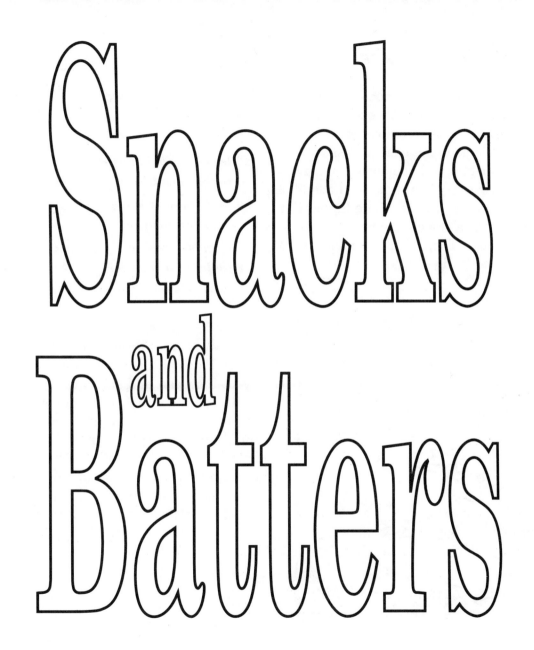

Lizzy's Crazy Cake

I have baked a lot of chocolate cakes in my time—fancy ones with exotic ingredients, lush ones with complicated steps, but none has equaled the ease and simplicity (and downright deliciousness) of Lizzy's Crazy Cake. Lizzy is a wonderful friend of mine with whom I cook. She adapted this recipe. It will take a child a few minutes to put together. The fragrant memory of making good food will keep forever.

1 mix all dry ingredients

2 oil water vinegar, vanilla
add liquids and mix

3 bake 375° 40min

What you will need:

3 cups flour

2 cups sugar

2 teaspoons baking soda

1 teaspoon salt

2 tablespoons cocoa powder

3/4 cup vegetable oil

1 teaspoon vanilla

2 tablespoons vinegar

2 cups cold water

Putting the cake together is as easy as one, two, three. Preheat oven to 375 degrees. Place all the dry ingredients in a 9-by-13-inch pan and stir with clean hands until well mixed. Make three holes in the dry mixture and place the oil in one hole, the vanilla and vinegar in the second hole, and the water in the third hole. Stir it all up together with a whisk. Bake for 40 minutes, or until the center springs back when you touch it lightly with your finger. Frost with your favorite icing.

Lotions, Potions, and Slime

Popovers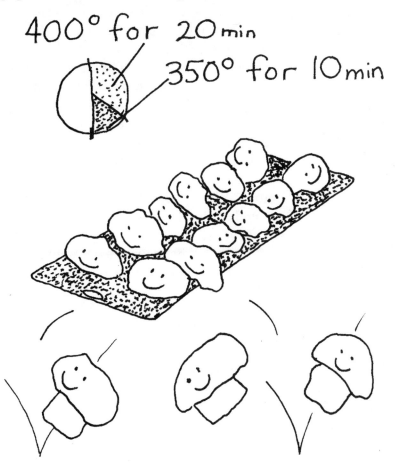

An old cookbook of mine calls these popovers "Bouncing Babies." And like magic this thin batter really does *pop* into delicious bouncing bites.

400° for 20 min

350° for 10 min

What you will need:

1 cup milk

1 cup white flour

1 teaspoon powdered sugar

1/2 teaspoon salt

4 eggs

Preheat oven to 400 degrees. Pour the milk into a bowl and whisk in the flour until there are no lumps. Add the sugar and salt. Vigorously beat the eggs in one at a time (kids are good at this). Oil a muffin tin or spray it with a baking spray. Pour the batter into the cups three-fourths full. Bake for 20 minutes, then lower the temperature to 350 and bake for another 10 minutes, until a deep golden brown. Serve them piping hot with powdered sugar and a squeeze of lemon juice.

Sourdough Starter

This recipe is half science and all heart. Who can resist hot-off-the-griddle sourdough pancakes? A jar of sourdough starter with the following recipe makes a great gift for the holidays.

What you will need:

3 cups flour

1 package active dry yeast

1¹/₂ cups hot water

2 cups milk (at room temperature)

In a medium bowl, combine 1 cup of the flour and the yeast. Stir in the hot water and mix until the lumps are worked out. Cover the bowl with a clean cloth and leave at room temperature for 24 hours. The next day, stir the mixture and leave it for another 12 hours. The yeast will be bubbling and brewing during this period. Your patience will be rewarded!

After the 12 hours, add the milk and the remaining 2 cups flour. Mix well with a wooden spoon. Cover the bowl with the cloth again and leave for another 24 hours. When the batter is properly proofed, it should be bubbly and have a delicious yeasty aroma.

You now have a basic sourdough sponge. Store loosely covered in the refrigerator in a glass container. We use the widemouthed canning jars—use wax paper instead of a lid and secure with the ring.

To keep your starter alive, stir at least once a week. For every 1 cup of starter used, replace with 1 cup flour and 1 cup warm water. Let the mixture set at room temperature until it bubbles, then return to the refrigerator.

Lotions, Potions, and Slime

Sourdough Hotcakes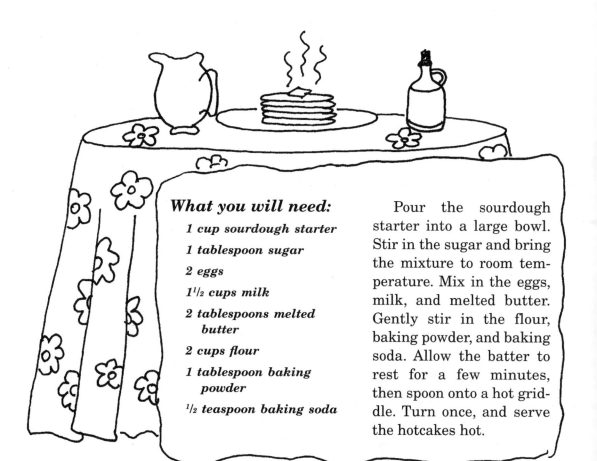

Now that you and your kids have that beautiful starter going, here is a most delicious way to use it.

What you will need:

- *1 cup sourdough starter*
- *1 tablespoon sugar*
- *2 eggs*
- *1½ cups milk*
- *2 tablespoons melted butter*
- *2 cups flour*
- *1 tablespoon baking powder*
- *½ teaspoon baking soda*

Pour the sourdough starter into a large bowl. Stir in the sugar and bring the mixture to room temperature. Mix in the eggs, milk, and melted butter. Gently stir in the flour, baking powder, and baking soda. Allow the batter to rest for a few minutes, then spoon onto a hot griddle. Turn once, and serve the hotcakes hot.

Cookie Paint

Keep this recipe because your family will want to use it over and over. Use the cookie recipe that follows this project, or paint your own favorite sugar cookie dough.

What you will need:

4 egg yolks

4 colors of food coloring

wax paper

cookie dough

empty 1-lb coffee can with the top and bottom taken out (file or press down any remaining sharp edges)

cotton swabs or clean paintbrushes

colored sugar crystals or sprinkles (optional)

Place the egg yolks in 4 separate small bowls. Add several drops of food coloring into 1 yolk and stir with a fork. Add more food coloring if necessary for a rich color. Use the same procedure with the remaining yolks, making different colors of paint with the food coloring.

For an easy cleanup afterwards, moisten a table top or counter and lay a strip of wax paper down (this keeps the paper from slipping). Roll the cookie dough onto the wax paper and use the coffee can as a cookie cutter to cut out big cookies. Place the cookie on a baking sheet with a large spatula. You are ready to paint! Using the swabs or paintbrushes, dip into the paint and spread it thickly over the cookie. Don't limit yourself! Paint a face, a farm, or a Picasso-like extravaganza of color and shapes. Sprinkle with sugar crystals if desired and bake as directed.

For even more fun, scramble up green eggs and ham with the leftover green paint and egg whites. Then read the book *Green Eggs and Ham* by Dr. Seuss while you munch.

A Very Special Sugar Cookie

What makes this recipe so special? It is a perfect recipe for kids: easy to make, no fuss, and delicious.

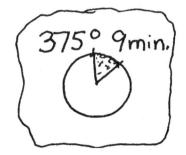

What you will need:

4 cups flour

2 teaspoons baking powder

1 teaspoon salt

³/₄ cup butter or margarine

1¹/₂ cups sugar

2 eggs

2 teaspoons vanilla

1 teaspoon lemon extract

Preheat oven to 375 degrees. Sift together the flour, baking powder, and salt into a bowl. In a separate bowl, cream the butter and sugar together until fluffy. Next beat in the eggs, vanilla, and lemon extract. Stir the flour mixture in by thirds until everything is incorporated. Dampen a counter or table top and lay out a strip of wax paper. Roll out the dough, cut out with cookie cutters, and lift carefully with a spatula onto a baking sheet. Bake until light brown, about 9 minutes.

Crash Cookies

Pull out this recipe when the kids feel that life is stupid and boring and awful and they just want to smack something. Pound away toward peace with delicious abandon, for the more they squeeze and squash, the better the cookie!

350° for 10 min.

What you will need:

- *3 cups oatmeal*
- *1½ cups flour*
- *1½ cups brown sugar*
- *1 teaspoon cinnamon*
- *½ teaspoon nutmeg*
- *1½ cups margarine*
- *1 teaspoon baking soda*

Preheat oven to 350 degrees. The directions are simple: place all the ingredients in a large bowl and knead, squeeze, squish, and rub everything together for as long as you want. Then drop walnut-sized pieces of dough onto an ungreased cookie sheet and bake for 10 minutes, or until done. Eat the cookies warm with a big glass of cold milk.

Lotions, Potions, and Slime

Soups

Soups are the most comforting of all kitchen potions. Whether it is a cold winter day or a slow afternoon, children love the chopping and stirring and aroma of a homemade soup. The following soups are two of our favorites.

Stone Soup

It was school vacation, and all I wanted was to spend one morning in the city at Seattle's Farmer's Market with my children. Just one measly morning. Almost-thirteen-year-old Jenna loves forays into Seattle, but our three lively boys feel the city is as complicated and pinched as a new pair of leather shoes. I prepared for a storm of protest. And it came. The boys immediately informed me that we couldn't possibly go—why waste the time? There were too many important things to do.

Like what? I stubbornly asked.

Like number one: Figure out a way to make a boat out of that old bathtub that washed up on the beach. Number two: Work on a totally camouflaged fort, and number three: Ride bikes and search for roadkill for the cemetery.

I looked at their intense faces and almost wavered, but I was prepared. We are going to go, I told them, because we are having Stone Soup for dinner tonight and I want you to choose the vegetables at the Market and make it yourselves.

This pricked their interest considerably. Stone Soup like in the book?

Yes. And Thunder Cake for dessert. (*Thunder Cake* is a delightful story where a wise grandmother helps a child overcome her fear of lightening with the making of a special cake. A delicious recipe follows at the end of the book.)

Now *this* was a curious proposition. Curious enough to sway their anchored minds my way and into the car. We read the wonderful book *Stone Soup* on the ferry into Seattle, and with the story fresh in our minds, we spent a leisurely morning at the Market picking out the vegetables: fresh peas, carrots, a fat potato. An onion, a few green beans, and celery. No tomatoes or green peppers—the boys decided upon radishes instead. I swallowed my protest.

When we arrived home later that afternoon, I was surprised how quickly the boys dropped the bathtub and roadkill undertakings. The imperative of Stone Soup drove them to leap out of the car and gather three large rocks from the yard. They scrubbed them hard in the sink and placed them in a big pot of water. There was a collective sigh of anticipation as the stones sank.

Everyone went to work. I never saw such industry in the kitchen! They peeled and chopped and diced and tasted and smelled and kept adding everything to the pot while I did nothing but watch. The soup began to simmer and bubble. Inviting smells filled the kitchen. This needs to cook for awhile, I told them, and their stirred up minds moved on to the bathtub boat problem. Alone in the kitchen, I surreptitiously added chicken broth, oregano, ground cumin, garlic, and a few chili pepper flakes.

Several hours later, we sat down to a feast: Stone Soup, fresh bread from the Market, slices of cheddar cheese, and the surprisingly luscious chocolate Thunder Cake. Although we didn't sing and dance into the night like the soldiers and villagers, a memory was made that would last a long time. And in this mother's mind, the conclusion of the book resonated deep and full: If one knows the recipe to Stone Soup, one will never starve. Neither by belly nor by heart.

Further Reading for Cooking by Stories:

Stone Soup, Marcia Brown

Thunder Cake, Patricia Polacco

Cloudy with a Chance of Meatballs, Judi Barret

Jamberry, Bruce Degen

Pancakes for Breakfast, Tomie De Paola

Blueberries for Sal, Robert McCloskey

If You Give a Moose a Muffin, Laura Joffe Numeroff

Alice in Wonderland, Lewis Carroll (the chapter when the Knave of Hearts is on trial for stealing strawberry tarts from the Queen—make strawberry tarts!)

Tom Sawyer, Mark Twain (make Tom's recipe for fried fish when Joe Harper and Huck run away)

Wild West Bean Soup Fixin's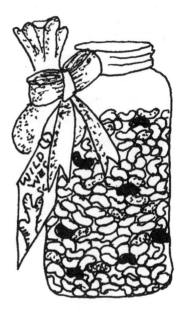

Have you ever scooped and run a thousand dried beans through your hands? It is an indescribably pleasant feeling! When they were toddlers my children's favorite rainy day activity was sorting, spooning, filling cups with, and swooshing little hands into the big bowl of beans I kept in the cupboard. Out of this, a project was born—a delicious gift as much fun to make as it is to give.

You can make an event out of selecting the beans for your soup. Our neighborhood grocery store carries a huge variety of dried beans in the bulk section. Beans with exciting names like rattlesnake, Appaloosa, red runner, and turtle. The type of bean does not particularly affect the taste of the soup. It is a heavenly recipe the whole family will enjoy with cornbread and grated cheese on a cold winter evening.

What you will need:

1 pound of a variety of dried beans

quart jar with a lid

ribbon

plastic wrap to make a small beribboned pouch of the following spices: 1/2 teaspoon ground cumin, 1/2 teaspoon ground chili, 1 teaspoon garlic granules, 1 teaspoon seasoning salt, 1/2 teaspoon thyme, a few chili pepper flakes (you can adjust the seasoning up or down to suit your taste)

Have your child place the beans in the jar. Place the lid on the jar. Cut out the following recipe and paste it on a decorated card. Paper punch a hole in the card, thread a ribbon through, and tie around the lid along with the packet of spices. Be sure to make this soup for your own family one day.

Wild West Bean Soup

What you will need:

1 quart jar of beans

8 slices of bacon, cut into pieces

2 quarts water

2 tablespoons vinegar

$1/2$ cup catsup

1 onion diced

1 4-ounce can diced chilies

1 tablespoon molasses

spice packet

The night before making the soup, cover the beans with water and soak. The next day, pour them in a colander, drain, and rinse. Place the beans in a big pot with the uncooked bacon and the 2 quarts of water. Cover and simmer for around an hour and a half. Add the remaining ingredients, including the contents of the spice packet, and simmer for another half hour. You may need to add a little extra water if the soup is too thick. Top with grated cheese or sour cream. Chopped fresh tomatoes are wonderful as a garnish, too.

Lotions, Potions, and Slime

Fruit-Flavored Popcorn Balls

Making popcorn balls is a snap with this easy recipe. Add dried fruit or peanuts for a special treat.

What you will need:

1 cup corn syrup

1/2 cup sugar

1 small box fruit-flavored gelatin

10 cups popcorn

butter

Stir the corn syrup and the sugar together in a pan. Bring to a boil and remove from the heat. Add the gelatin and stir until dissolved. Place the popcorn in a big bowl and pour the gelatin mixture over the popcorn. Toss everything together until the popcorn is coated. Butter your hands and form the popcorn into balls.

POPCORN BALLS DON'T BOUNCE BUT YOU CAN'T EAT A TENNIS BALL!

Finger Jell-O

The dense, jiggly nature of this treat is a sure hit for kids. It even packs well in school lunches and is fat free.

What you will need:

2 large packages of Jell-O (any flavor)

2¹/₂ cups boiling apple juice (or water)

cookie cutters

Place the Jell-O in a large bowl and pour in the apple juice. Stir until the mixture is dissolved. Pour into a 9-by-13-inch pan and refrigerate several hours until firm. Use the cookie cutters to cut shapes in the Jell-O. To remove, briefly place the bottom of the pan in warm water and use a spatula to gently lift the shapes out.

Lotions, Potions, and Slime

Wiggly Jiggly Gelatin Eggs

"x" of tape over the small hole

large hole end

What in the world is that?! my son asked when he beheld the emerald green egg we had made. These are beautiful and bright as a rainbow. Nest several in different colors on a bed of lettuce for a side dish at dinner.

What you will need:

6 eggs

1¹/₂ cups water

2 packets unflavored gelatin

1 small package of fruit-flavored gelatin

masking tape

Carefully tap a dime-sized hole at the narrow end of each egg, and a much smaller hole at the other end (I use a carving fork prong). Blow out the contents of the egg from the small hole into a bowl (save for scrambled eggs). Rinse the egg shell with warm water and drain.

Pour the water into a pot and stir in both the unflavored and flavored gelatin. Mix well and bring to a boil. When the gelatin completely dissolves, remove from the heat.

While the gelatin cools, tape the small hole closed on the eggs with masking tape. Make an *X* out of the tape and press gently but firmly to seal the tape completely to the egg shell. Set the eggs in an egg carton.

Pour the gelatin while it is still warm and runny into the eggs using a small funnel. Refrigerate for several hours until firm.

If you do not have a small funnel to pour the gelatin into the eggs, you can make one from a plastic milk jug or carton. Cut an approximate 6-by-8-inch rectangle from the jug and form a funnel. Tape it together.

When ready to crack these beauties open, run the shell under warm water to loosen the gelatin from the inner shell. Peel carefully.

Jelly Fish Bowls

An amusing treat or a fun party favor. Make a batch of these with your child when a fishy theme is called for.

What you will need:

1 large box blueberry-flavored gelatin

2 cups hot water

1 cup cold water

1 cup ice cubes

6 clear plastic cups

gummy fish

Pour the gelatin into a bowl that has a pouring spout (a pitcher will work, too) and add the hot water. Stir until completely dissolved. Add the cold water and the ice, and stir until the gelatin thickens. Remove any ice that hasn't melted. Pour the gelatin into the cups and gently place the gummy fish in the cups. If the gelatin is too thin to suspend the fish, refrigerate 15 minutes or more to thicken it. Of course, this sweet-toothed family of mine added a squirt of canned whipping cream, insisting it looked like the foam on waves!

Lotions, Potions, and Slime

Chocolate Leaves

You will be amazed at the beautiful details that emerge on your leaves—*every vein and line in chocolate!* We love this project. Chocolate leaves make elegant cake decorations, too. (Read the safety note, but don't let it squash this project.)

What you will need:

dozen camellia or magnolia leaves
(or other heavy, waxy-type leaf)

1 cup chocolate chips

clean medium-sized paintbrush

Be safe! Camellia and magnolia leaves are safe to use, but before you use any part of a plant, be sure you know whether or not it's toxic. Even though the leaf is not ingested in this project, accidental poisoning is a real childhood danger. Your local poison control center's education division (see your phone book) can help you to determine if a plant is safe to use.

Clean the surface of the leaves with a warm wet dishcloth. Lay a piece of wax paper on a cookie sheet. Next melt the chocolate chips in a microwave oven on high power for 1 minute, then stir. Continue to melt and stir the chips at 20-second intervals, until completely melted. If you do not have a microwave, melt the chocolate chips on the stove in a double boiler or heavy-bottomed pan over medium heat.

Are you ready to paint? Hold a leaf by the stem, and paint a thick layer of melted chocolate on its surface. Lay it on the wax paper. Continue with the remaining leaves. Place them in the refrigerator until firm. When the leaves are ready, gently pull down a stem and lift the chocolate from the leaf.

Apple Candy

This is a recipe for the apple candy that made Washington State famous. We like this homemade version better than the store-bought variety.

What you will need:

- 2½ *cups applesauce*
- 4 *envelopes plain gelatin*
- 4 *cups sugar*
- 2 *teaspoons vanilla*
- 1½ *cups broken walnuts (optional)*
- 2 *teaspoons lemon juice*
- *powdered sugar*

Place 1 cup of the applesauce in a heavy saucepan. Stir the gelatin into the applesauce and leave it for 10 minutes. Next mix in the sugar and the remaining applesauce and place over medium heat. Cook for 15 minutes, stirring occasionally. Remove from the heat and add the vanilla, nuts, and lemon juice. Pour into a buttered 9-by-13-inch pan and place in the refrigerator. When the candy has set up, cut into squares and roll each square in powdered sugar.

AN APPLE A DAY KEEPS THE DOCTOR AWAY!

WITH NUTS

ONLY POWDERED SUGAR

Lotions, Potions, and Slime

Summertime Slush

Make this yummy slush in the morning with your children. Eat it nice and slow in the cool shade of a hot afternoon.

What you will need:

- *2 12-oz cans of frozen fruit juice concentrate, thawed (pick your favorite flavor*
- *1 32-oz bottle of clear soda pop (7-Up, ginger ale, or Mountain Dew)*
- *small paper cups or zipper-top sandwich bags*

Mix together the thawed fruit concentrate with the soda pop. Ladle ½ cup of the mixture into each paper cup or sandwich bag and place in the freezer. Makes approximately a dozen treats.

Snow Ice Cream

My grandmother made this treat for her family during the Depression, when ice cream was an unheard-of luxury. When snow arrived in their small Idaho town, the children rejoiced: time to make snow ice cream!

What you will need:

1¹/₂ cups half-and-half

2 teaspoons vanilla

¹/₂ cup sugar

salt

2 quarts clean fresh snow

chocolate syrup

Pour the half-and-half, vanilla, and sugar in a bowl. Whisk together and add a pinch of salt. Quickly stir in snow until the mixture reaches ice cream consistency. Spoon into bowls, add chocolate syrup, and enjoy.

Lotions, Potions, and Slime

Strawberry Snow Ice Cream

This recipe is our hands-down favorite. You can omit the eggs if desired (the ice cream will not taste as rich).

What you will need:

2 eggs (optional, but we prefer them)

³/4 cup sugar

1 cup evaporated milk (or low-fat evaporated milk)

1 teaspoon vanilla

1 10-oz package frozen sweetened strawberries, thawed

bowl of clean fresh snow

Whip the eggs in a large bowl. Add the sugar, milk, and vanilla, then stir in the thawed strawberries with the juice. Fold in clean snow until the mixture reaches ice cream consistency. Eat immediately!

Tasty Beast Treats

Making pet treats is an activity that never dies around here. We have made these treats for years and believe they are better than anything you can buy. Remember your favorite creatures on their birthdays or for the holidays!

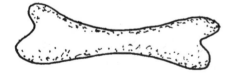

Fish Snaps for Dogs

What started out as a kitty treat turned into the most irresistible snap snack for dogs. These are great for training sessions. Use them as a reward for good behavior.

What you will need:

1 package dry yeast

¹/₂ cup warm water

¹/₂ cup bran

1 cup whole-wheat flour

1 cup white flour

¹/₄ cup cornmeal

1 teaspoon salt

1 small can tuna fish in oil

¹/₂ cup dried milk

dog cookie

Preheat oven to 325 degrees. Dissolve the yeast in the warm water. Mix the dry ingredients together in a large bowl. Add the undrained tuna, yeast, and milk to the dry mixture and stir or squeeze the dough in your hands until well mixed. If the dough seems too dry, add a little water; too sticky, add more flour. Roll the dough out to ¼ inch thick. Use cookie cutters to cut dog bones or other shapes from the dough and place on a baking sheet. Bake for 30 minutes.

Horse Cookies

What you will need:

1 cup molasses

¹/₂ cup oil

3¹/₂ cups whole-wheat flour

1 cup grated carrot

Preheat oven to 350 degrees. Stir the molasses and oil together. Add the flour and the grated carrot. Drop by spoonfuls on a greased cookie sheet and bake for 12–15 minutes. These treats aren't bad for humans either!

Carrot-shaped

horse cookie yum!

Jenna's Power Cupcakes for the Birds

What you will need:

1 cup beef suet (ask your butcher) or shortening

1/2 cup Grape-nuts cereal

1 cup birdseed

1 cup coarse cornmeal

1/2 cup bread crumbs

raisins (optional)

paper cupcake holders

muffin tin

chopsticks or pencils

cotton thread

Melt the suet or the shortening on the stove in a heavy pan. Stir in the remaining ingredients (any combination of these ingredients can be used). Place the cupcake holders in the muffin tin and press the mixture into the holders. To make a hole for hanging the cupcakes, use a chopstick or pencil and push it into the center of the cupcake. Allow the cupcakes to firm up, then remove the chopstick and the cupcake holder. Thread a length of cotton string through the hole in the cupcake and hang from a tree branch.

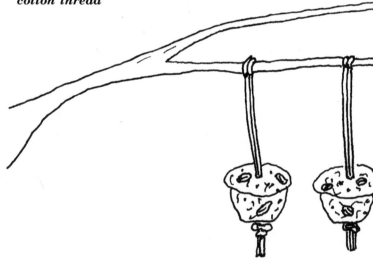

Lotions, Potions, and Slime

Jessa's Butterfly Pie

When Jessa (a very dear friend of mine) was a girl she used to get in trouble for sneaking sugar out of the house for these magical pies. She alone knew the secret recipe for attracting butterflies—until now.

What you will need:

dirt

water

flower petals

1 cup sugar

pie tin

a sunny day

Mix dirt and water together to get a nice mud mixture. Stir in lots of flower petals and the sugar. Put the mixture in a pie tin and set it out in the sun to dry. Count the butterflies that enjoy your creation!

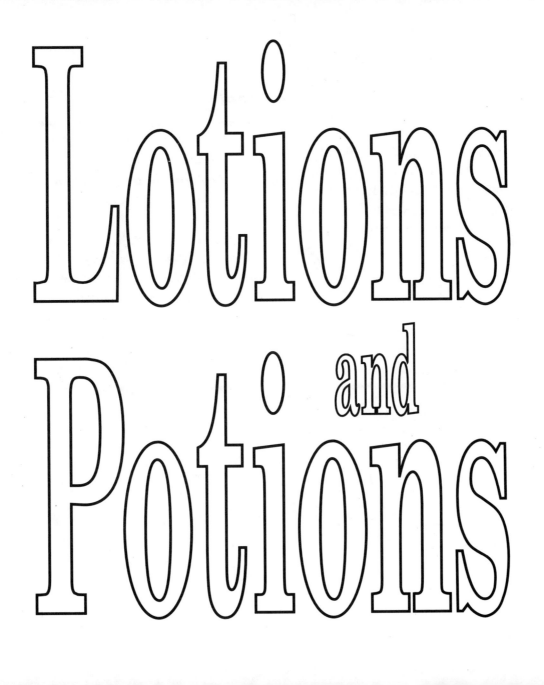

Rub-a-Dub-Tub Paint

Whenever I was fed up with my toddlers' cranky moods, I ran a warm bath for them, even if it was the middle of the day. Today I send my teenagers to the tub with the same results: a calm and clean human being emerges ready to face life again. Add this soap paint to the operation and you have the ingredients for restorative fun at any age.

What you will need:

1 cup mild soap flakes (available in the detergent section of your grocer)

5 tablespoons water

food coloring or tempera paint

zipper-top sandwich bags

Place the soap flakes in a bowl. Add the water and then a few drops of food coloring or paint. Beat the mixture together with an electric beater until it reaches the consistency of whipped cream. Make a few batches of different colored soap paint and place in plastic bags and seal. When ready to use, snip the corner of the bag and squeeze the paint out.

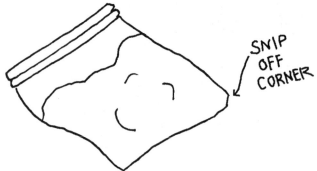

SNIP OFF CORNER

Handmade Bath Salts

Shopping for the sweetest smelling essential oil is half the fun of this project. Your local bath and soap specialty shop carries a wide variety to choose from.

What you will need:

4 tablespoons baking soda

essential oil

food coloring

Measure the baking soda into a bowl, then add a few drops of essential oil and a few drops of food coloring. Mash together with the back of a spoon until the ingredients are completely incorporated.

Decorate envelopes to place the salts in, or place in a pretty jar with illustrated instructions tied around the lid. These aromatic salts in a hot bath restore the soundness of mind and spirit on a stressful day.

Bath Tea

Thyme is a strong medicinal herb long used as an expectorant for tight, dry coughs. Thyme also promotes the healing of skin inflammations and "strengthens nerves." But I just like the smell of it in my bath. So do the kids. Place the tea in a pretty jar with a lid. Bath tea makes a great gift, too.

What you will need:

 2 quarts water

 2 cups dried thyme
  (you can substitute dried peppermint or rosemary)

Bring the water to a boil in a large pan. Add the dried thyme and bring the mixture back to a boil. Cover the pot with a lid and remove from heat. Steep for 15 minutes. Strain through a sieve into a pitcher. Use it immediately in a hot bath, or save in a covered container until needed.

Lotions, Potions, and Slime

Foaming Bath Oil

This is an all-natural bubble bath that soothes and softens your skin as you soak. Foaming bath oil makes a great gift along with a thick washcloth and a magazine (or comic book) to read in the tub.

What you will need:

³/₄ cup vegetable oil

3 tablespoons mild white dish-washing liquid (there are several varieties of natural, biodegradable dish soap available at your grocer)

food coloring

2 tablespoons witch hazel (available at your pharmacy)

several drops of essential oil (available at bath and perfume shops) or extract (lemon or orange, at your grocer)

nice jar with a lid

1 egg white (to keep ingredients from separating)

Place all the ingredients except the egg white in the jar, and replace the lid. Shake thoroughly to mix. Add the egg white, shake again. Make a pretty label for the jar. Use several tablespoons of the bath oil mixed into your bath. Keeps well in the refrigerator.

Grit Soap on a Rope

Save your soap slivers, or use all those motel soaps your kids have collected over the years. We hang our grit soap by the utility sink to clean off the grimy evidence of outdoor adventures (and it works just beautifully).

What you will need:

¹/₂ cup soap pieces

¹/₂ cup cornmeal

2 tablespoons vegetable oil

few drops essential oil or lemon extract

1 tablespoon warm water

long piece of raffia, string, or twine

Place the soap pieces and cornmeal in a blender and pulverize everything into a coarse powder. Place the powder in a bowl and add the oil, scent, and water. Mash everything together with your hands. Form the soap with the raffia or twine down the center. We found a lemon shape was the most useful. When the soap is dry, it is ready to use.

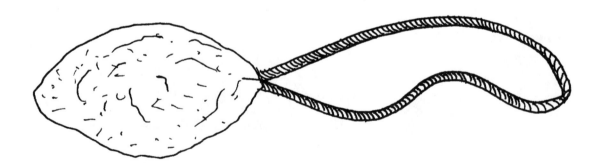

Lotions, Potions, and Slime

Lemon After-Bath Splash

This old-fashioned recipe is a stimulating potion to cool and refresh the skin. Your child will love both ends of this project: making it and using it—and don't forget to make a batch for yourself!

What you will need:

½ cup herbal lemon tea (nice and strong), cooled

½ cup witch hazel (available at your pharmacy)

1 tablespoon glycerine (available at your pharmacy)

1 teaspoon lemon extract

small jar with a lid

Place all the ingredients in the jar and shake until well mixed. Make a label for the jar or use a canning label. Use after bathing or simply to refresh your skin on a hot day (this splash is particularly cooling if kept in the refrigerator).

Homemade Sunscreen

Zinc oxide has long been used as an inexpensive and effective sunscreen. Slathered on thick and full strength, it offers excellent sun protection. Here's a simple recipe you can make with your child that offers an alternative to the harsh chemicals in store-bought sunscreen. Keep in mind that you need to apply this sunscreen more often than you do commercial sunscreens.

PROTECT YOUR SKIN FROM SOLAR RAYS

What you will need:

1 teaspoon zinc oxide (available at your pharmacy)

1 tablespoon olive oil

Measure the zinc oxide and olive oil into a bowl. Use a fork to mix the ingredients together completely. Just before going outdoors, rub a heavy amount of sunscreen on. Reapply frequently, particularly after coming in contact with water.

Fountain of Foam

This is a toddler activity that even older kids enjoy!

What you will need:

> *dish-washing soap*
>
> *water*
>
> *food coloring (optional)*
>
> *old-fashioned egg beater or whisk*

Squirt a dash or two of dish-washing soap into a bowl full of water. Add a few drops of food coloring if desired. Give your child the soapy solution along with the old-fashioned egg beater (the kind you turn by hand) or wire whisk to churn the solution into a mountain of soft foam.

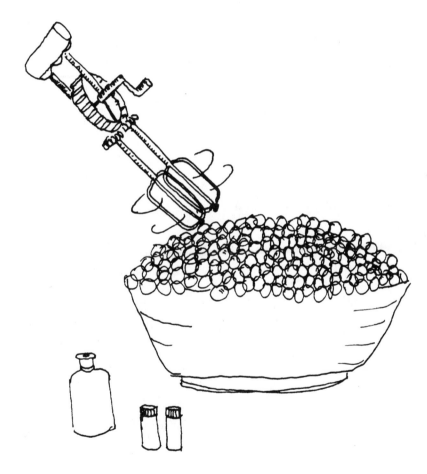

Paint Your Wagon! ✋

Or anything else your toddler desires! My own busy children loved this activity when they were young.

What you will need:
plastic bucket of water

large sponge paintbrush

Give your child the plastic bucket of water and paintbrush. He can enjoy "painting" everything from fences to wagons to the sides of the house.

GIVE YOUR SNOWMAN A HAWAIIAN SHIRT!

Snow Paint ✋

Turn your yard into a work of art!

What you will need:
3 spray bottles

water

food coloring
  (in 3 different colors)

Fill spray bottles with water. Add a tablespoon of food coloring to each bottle, and shake it up. Send your child out to spray the snow with rainbows of color.

Lotions, Potions, and Slime

Fake Blood

Don't throw away my blood! my son yelled at me. Now that is an interesting sentence, I thought to myself, as I rummaged through the refrigerator. This recipe looks remarkably like the real thing. My son used his batch for a home movie called *Crime Doesn't Pay*.

What you will need:

1/2 cup corn syrup

1 teaspoon red food coloring

few drops blue food coloring

Pour the corn syrup into a jar and add the food coloring. Stir it up. There you have it! Put a lid on the jar and it will keep for several weeks in the refrigerator. Like most food coloring spills, fake blood may be difficult to wash off fabric surfaces when dried. Clean fake blood up while fresh for best results.

Monstercide

It seems every child goes through a phase when *real* monsters are hidden in the house (under the bed, in the closets)—monsters that only your child can see. It's no use talking him out of it, this only confirms your child's worst fear: the monsters are only after *him*.

What you will need:

empty spray bottle

water

1 teaspoon almond extract

3 drops of blue food coloring

Fill the bottle with water and add the almond extract. Monsters *hate* the smell of almond extract. It smells exactly like the stinkiest stink in the world to them. They avoid it at all costs. Next drop in 3 drops of the blue food coloring. This is the secret ingredient. Blue is a color that hurts a monster to even glance at. Even though you will not see the blue when it is sprayed, monsters can detect even a molecule of blue with their beady eyes. When they see it, they run as far away as possible. Shake everything all up. Ready?

Use the spray in all the places monsters like to lurk (under beds, in closets, behind doors). It may take several days of spraying to rid the house of the beasties, but I have never known monstercide to fail. Good luck.

Index

WANT TO DO MORE COOL STUFF?

THE MUDPIES ACTIVITY BOOK
Recipes for Invention
Nancy Blakey

Parents, teachers, daycare providers—anyone with a child to entertain—will love this kid-sized sourcebook packed with creative ideas. Using simple materials you can find around the house or classroom, here's a book that proves that fun and learning can go hand in hand.
144 pages, paperback

PRETEND SOUP and Other Real Recipes
A Cookbook for Preschoolers and Up
Mollie Katzen and Ann Henderson

Best-selling vegetarian cookbook author teams up with an early childhood education specialist, and guess what happens? A lively, colorful book that lets kids as young as three be the chef, while an adult acts as guide and helper.

"An unusually accessible, attractive, process-oriented cookbook...with imaginative and appealing recipes."—*Horn Book*
96 pages, hardcover

MORE MUDPIES
101 Alternatives to Television
Nancy Blakey

Based on materials you can easily find around the house or classroom, the projects in this sequel include homemade face paint, a family cookbook, science activities, beach candles, and much, much more.
144 pages, paperback

ALL THE BEST CONTESTS FOR KIDS
5th Edition
Joan M. Bergstrom, Ed.D. and Craig Bergstrom

Completely updated and revised, this handy book includes hundreds of contests for kids to enter, in fields from art to computers to sewing to roller skating. Entry information given for every contest, plus hints for starting your own contest, or getting your writing and artwork published.

Winner of a 1990 Parent's Choice Award.
288 pages, paperback

HEARTS & CRAFTS
Sheri Brownrigg

Here's a collection of crafts and recipes that is sure to please that fanciful, whimsical, and gushily-romantic side to us all. From Lavender Wands to Red Hot Cinnamon Tea, here's a unique book containing crafts kids can make and enjoy all year 'round.
96 pages, paperback

THE BEST SUMMER EVER
A Parents' Guide
Joan M. Bergstrom, Ed.D.

Here's the why and how of planning, carrying out, and enjoying one of the most precious times in a school-age child's life—summertime. Complete with a section of handy organizational tools ready for photocopying to keep this important task easy on parents.
112 pages, paperback

ONE HUNDRED WONDERFUL THINGS TO KEEP KIDS BUSY AND HAVING FUN
Pam Schiller and Joan Rossano

Activities of all kinds for school-aged kids to do alone or in groups. This is a wonderful resource for daycare leaders, grandparents, or anyone who's ever heard "I'm bored—there's nothing to do."
88 pages, paperback

For more information, or to order, call Tricycle Press at the number below. We accept VISA, MasterCard, and American Express. You may also write for our free complete catalog of books, posters, and audiotapes for kids and their grown-ups.

TRICYCLE PRESS
P.O. Box 7123
Berkeley, California 94707
1-800-841-BOOK